The Tycoon's Revenge

Baby for the Billionaire — Book One

By Melody Anne

COPYRIGHT

Powerful, Loyal, Unforgettable
Follow the Titans
as they find true love

The Tycoon's Revenge
Baby for the Billionaire Series
Book One

DEDICATION

This book is dedicated to my son, Johnathan, who brings me so much joy. He always makes me laugh and I'm proud of him every single day. He's truly one in a million and my life wouldn't be the same without him in it. I love you, Johnathan.

NOTE FROM THE AUTHOR

THIS IS THE beginning of the Titan series. I love to write family romance books because I think the family aspect is just as important as the romance itself. My life would truly be lonely without my family. I love them and would do anything for them. I wanted the Titans to be cousins because I love many of my cousins as if they were my siblings. My cousin Tracy used to do my hair and makeup all the time when I was a kid. She made me formal dresses and then, when she could drive, she'd take me around. I remember how great I thought it was that my way-cool older cousin thought I was special enough to be with her. I idolized her as a child. To tell you the truth, I still do. She's gorgeous and funny, and she can do anything, from sewing and hair to putting in her own floors and cabinets. She's superwoman.

I have many other fond memories of my family, and I'll use some of those experiences in the different books I write. I hope you grow to love the Titans as much as the Andersons. I love my male leads to be strong, powerful men, and I love the

Cinderella story.

Thank you, as always, to all the people who inspire me every day to keep on writing, and for all your wonderful comments and reviews. I love to hear from my fans and try to answer every question. The best way to reach me is through Facebook, which I have listed here. I love having conversations with all of you and I love knowing what you think.

Melody Anne

BOOKS BY MELODY ANNE

BILLIONAIRE BACHELORS

*The Billionaire Wins the Game

*The Billionaire's Dance

*The Billionaire Falls

*The Billionaire's Marriage Proposal

*Blackmailing the Billionaire

*Runaway Heiress

*The Billionaire's Final Stand

*Unexpected Treasure

*Holiday Treasure

BABY FOR THE BILLIONAIRE

+The Tycoon's Revenge

+The Tycoon's Vacation

+The Tycoon's Proposal

+The Tycoon's Secret

+The Lost Tycoon – **Coming Soon**

RISE OF THE DARK ANGEL

-Midnight Fire – Rise of the Dark Angel – Book One

-Midnight Moon – Rise of the Dark Angel – Book Two

-Midnight Storm – Rise of the Dark Angel – Book Three

-Midnight Rising – Rise of the Dark Angel – Book Four –

Coming Soon

Surrender

=Surrender – Book One

=Submit – Book Two

=Seduced – Book Three

=Scorched – Book Four

CONTACT MELODY ANNE

www.facebook.com/melodyanneauthor
www.melodyanne.com
Twitter @authmelodyanne

PROLOGUE

A STAR FELL from the heavens and Jasmine watched in awe as the light slowly dimmed, and then disappeared entirely.

The feel of Derek's hand stroking her back was pure bliss, and she felt as if she could lie here all night long, never return to the real world. This place they'd created together was perfect — no father telling her it was wrong, no worries, no troubles.

"I love you so much, Jasmine," Derek whispered in her ear. "You are my world, my life."

"You know how much I love you," she replied, lifting her head to accept the gentle kiss from his lips. Her body melted all over again at his slightest touch.

"I hate having to take you back home tonight," he said, pulling her even closer.

"Then don't," she begged.

"Your father would hunt us down," he told her.

"I don't care. I know what I want and that's to be with you, Derek."

"Then we should run away together. I've actually been thinking about it a lot, about moving on from here." As she flinched, he added, "Only with you, my love; I'd never leave you behind. Here's my idea. My dad will be fine. He's starting his new business. It's foolproof. He wants me to run it with him, but I have bigger dreams than running a computer store. I want to go to the city, intern for someone like Bill Gates, learn from them, and make something of myself," he said, passion flowing through his young voice.

"You already are someone special, Derek. You won my heart, and I've given it to you for life," she said, kissing his neck as the full moon washed its light over their naked bodies.

"You make me feel special — make me feel as if there's nothing I can't do."

"That's because you're Superman," she told him with a giggle. "Definitely more powerful than a locomotive…"

He laughed, then grew serious again. "What do you say? I'll take care of you if you come with me. We can get married and start our lives in the city," he promised. "You can even go to cooking school and open that café you've always talked about." He grew more excited as he spoke.

Jasmine paused as she thought about what he was asking of her. Could she leave it all behind? If Derek left, though, what would she have to stay for? Nothing worth keeping. She loved her father, but he was so cold most of the time — how much would he miss her, really? He'd eventually get over his anger and their relationship would heal, though it might take a few years.

Derek would have to come back. His father and cousins

were here, and they were all closer than most families. The three boys were more siblings than cousins. She'd just be starting a new adventure with the boy she loved, but she wouldn't be cutting her ties here completely.

"Yes. I'll come with you. You have to give me a few days, though," she asked.

Derek pulled her on top of him with a laugh. Jasmine was a little sore, but the pleasure far outweighed the discomfort. The two of them made love beneath the stars, their joy shining even brighter.

They were going to forge a new path for just the two of them. Nothing could keep them from their destiny.

CHAPTER ONE

Ten Years Later

ANOTHER NIGHT, ANOTHER party, though for once probably not another woman. Derek Titan looked around the crowded room and forced himself not to yawn. He couldn't stand attending events where everyone drank too much, laughed too loud and tried far too hard to impress one another.

Derek knew he was what women considered a real catch. Hell, an idiotic magazine had published a write-up on Seattle's most eligible bachelors and ranked him, with his picture, as number one. He'd been furious and had tried to have himself taken out of the article, but his attorney had spouted some crap about freedom of speech. OK, so there were good points in the First Amendment, but he hadn't seen many. Since the article appeared, even more women with their eyes on a prize had approached him.

The magazine listed his net worth as equal to Bill Gates'.

Though slightly exaggerated, that part at least was related to business. But of what possible interest or relevance was the hackneyed phrase "tall, dark and handsome"? So what if he stood over six feet and had broad shoulders? He gagged when he read of "rippling muscles." The flipping author even gave advice on how to meet him: don't bother with stalking him at the gym — he hated those places — but take up running, because he ran every morning, and sometimes in the evenings too, as a way to relieve stress.

Though it hinted, at least the article didn't quite say what happened after his second-best way to relieve stress. But here it was — the minute he'd finished taking a woman to bed, he just walked away, and that wasn't something to inspire the magazine's female readership. Sure, a lot of his women tried to get him to stay, but no one held his interest longer than it took him to zip up his pants.

He'd let a woman beat him once at the mating game. And after Jasmine shattered his heart and destroyed his father's business venture, he'd lost interest in the female sex — except, of course, for the sex. His priority had long been revenge. He figured that once he got it, he'd think about settling down.

A woman breezed by him wearing entirely too much perfume, and he snapped back to reality. He sighed, then grabbed a glass of wine from a passing waiter.

These parties were all about who had the most to offer. The women were on the prowl, and the men were fishing. He just wasn't interested.

He watched as a couple of superficial wannabe socialites passed by in low-cut gowns, dripping with diamonds. They were trying to catch his eye, and normally he'd make their day by flirting a little, giving them the impression they stood a chance. Today wasn't that day. He had a raging headache, and he was pissed that he'd been summoned to this snooze-fest.

"There you are, boy. What are you doing hiding in the corner?" Daniel Titan, his father, had walked up to give him the third degree.

"I'm wondering why I'm here when I'd rather be home with a scotch and my feet up," Derek replied.

"You're here because you received a request from your father. I have some things to discuss with you later," Daniel said in his no-nonsense voice.

"And it couldn't wait?" Derek questioned.

"Oh, live a little. You're always so busy adding megabucks to your bank account that you don't stop to smell the cabernet sauvignon," his father said.

"I live it up plenty. Hell, I was in Milan last week."

"You were in Milan on business. That doesn't count," his dad told him.

"For me, the ideal time is mixing business with pleasure," Derek said with a waggle of his eyebrows. Both men relaxed. "Seriously, Dad, I do have a headache. What's so important it couldn't wait until tomorrow morning?"

Once Derek had made his first million, he'd moved his father to the city. Daniel, now the chief financial officer of his huge corporation, had been instrumental in the company's swift and exponential growth. But his dad had gone through hard times more than once while Derek was growing up.

"David Freeman's here tonight, and he's talking to some

people, trying to get new investors," Daniel said, his eyes narrowing slightly as he looked at the man who'd destroyed his livelihood some years before.

Derek was on instant alert. He searched the room, spotting his enemy. David was the one who'd made Derek the cutthroat businessman he was. "It's far too late for him. By tomorrow morning, he'll know that his company is mine, no matter what he tries tonight," Derek said.

Derek saw a beautiful woman approach David, stepping up on her tiptoes to kiss him on the cheek. David didn't even bother to turn and acknowledge her. The man noticed nothing around him if it didn't have dollar signs on it, not even his stunning daughter.

Derek's eyes narrowed to slits. He hadn't seen Jasmine for ten years, and those years had been very good to her. It wasn't at all what he'd been expecting, although, with her supreme shallowness, he should have known she'd have focused first and foremost on her appearance.

The top of her dress hugged her body, dipping low in both the front and back. Her curves were even more pronounced now that her body had matured. Her gleaming dark hair was swept up in a classic bun, with tendrils floating around her delicate face. Her chocolate eyes had once mesmerized him. They had a hypnotic quality, with a deceptive innocence shining through the thick lashes.

His gut tightened at just the sight of her, and that outraged him. Was he still a complete fool about her? She'd nearly destroyed his entire family, and yet he still wanted her. But that was all right. After all, his full revenge included her; he would have her in his bed again, and then she'd be begging him not to leave. Shrinks might call it closure. To him, everything was far more primitive.

"I'm leaving now, Dad. There's nothing he can do tonight, and tomorrow's a busy day for me," Derek said. After clasping his father's hand, he turned away and walked from the room without once looking back.

CHAPTER TWO

JASMINE SPOTTED DEREK across the room, and fire and ice waged war within her. How dare he walk around as if he owned the place? She knew the kinder, gentler side of him, but that boy was long gone. He probably never really existed beyond her girlish imagination.

The man she'd spotted tonight wasn't the boy who had taken her virginity and promised her forever. She wished she could forget that summer so many years ago when she'd waited at the abandoned church all day, waited and waited, hoping something had happened to make him late. As the sun had faded from the sky, she'd finally had to admit he wasn't coming. It had all been lies.

Just as her father had said, Derek had told her all he needed to get her to have sex with him. Once he'd added her to his list of conquests, he'd been finished with her. The remembered pain was almost too much to bear, even ten years later.

She watched him turning and walking from the room. He was by far the sexiest man at the party, with his custom tuxedo and piercing blue eyes. Although he sat in an office all day, his body betrayed no hint of softness. Her heart fluttered as she dwelled again on those long summer nights of touching and tasting those hard muscles.

Derek disappeared around the corner just as he'd disappeared that summer ten years before. Back then, she'd believed in fairy tales and magic.

No more.

Jasmine had grown up very wealthy in a small town outside of Seattle, Washington. Her father owned a multimillion-dollar medical-equipment company, and she'd always had more than most people could ever hope for.

Her mother had died while giving birth to her, and her father never remarried. He dated a lot of women, but none of them really acknowledged her existence, so she didn't grow attached to any of them. Sometimes, Jasmine had thought it would be nice to have a woman help her pick out a dress or teach her how to do her hair. But the staff, at least, always spoiled her a bit, which she knew irritated her father.

She'd seen Derek in school from the time she was young, but she got to know him only the summer before her senior year in high school. His family was dirt poor, but he was always determined to make a success out of his life and turn things around. He ended up helping her with math, and soon they were fast friends. She'd loved his hunger and motivation and the way he never talked down about anyone. She thought he was every one of her fairy-tale heroes come to life.

Soon, she found she was spending every waking moment with him. When her father found out she was dating a boy from the poor side of town, he'd been furious and demanded that she end the relationship. It was the first time in her life her father told her she couldn't have something she wanted. It also was the first time she'd defied him.

She'd continued to see Derek behind her father's back. She loved that Derek seemed to like her for who she was and not for her money. He wouldn't let her spend money on him — ever. He worked hard for a construction company, which would frustrate her at times because she wanted him to be with her and not at a job. He'd laugh at her frustration, but he always made it up to her on the weekends.

"Jasmine?"

Jasmine turned to find that she'd completely tuned out of the conversation. Normally, she was the epitome of cool — making sure to schmooze with her father's investors. That was her job at these functions.

More than once she'd had to fend off the advances of some dirty old man. It was a source of contention between her father and her — just one of many.

She wouldn't sell her soul to the devil, even if the devil was dressed in a hand-tailored business suit. Money had its uses, and she certainly needed a lot more than she had, but she wasn't for sale, not at any price.

"I'm sorry. I have a slight headache tonight and it's made me lose focus," she answered sweetly to the sixty-year-old who was leering at her. She had to fight the shiver threatening to travel down her spine at the lust in his eyes.

"I was just telling your father that I would love to have the two of you up to my lake house sometime real soon."

No way in hell! That is what she wanted to say.

"That sounds like a very pleasant weekend. Make sure you have my father notify me of when," she answered instead, already planning a convenient illness.

The man beamed at her; his hand came up to rest on her upper arm, and then his finger trailed downward.

"Excuse me. I need some medicine for this annoying headache," she said, discreetly extracting herself from the man's slimy grip and walking away. She was on the verge of being sick. How many more of these functions would she have to attend before she'd had enough?

Seeing Derek tonight had been too much. Wasn't time supposed to heal all wounds? In her case, ten years obviously hadn't been enough time. Seeing her first love — the only man she'd ever loved — was just too much.

It was time to leave.

Tomorrow would be a better day. That had become her motto for the last decade. One of these days, maybe it would.

As she walked from the party, Jasmine thought back to the day that her innocence had been stolen from her, the day that she'd realized she couldn't trust her heart, and she certainly couldn't trust men…

CHAPTER THREE

ARRIVING HOME AFTER being out all night, Jasmine felt her knees shaking. As she stepped through the doorway, her father was standing there, his face blotched with color, and spittle flying from his lips.

"I love him, Dad," she said, firming her shoulders as she faced down the man who instilled the very meaning of the word *fear* inside her.

"You don't know what love is. You are only seventeen," he shouted, stepping closer.

For the first time, she feared he might strike her. He'd never been a caring or engaged parent, but he'd never physically abused her.

"We're going to get married." She knew she couldn't just run away now. If she wanted to be a grown-up, then she needed to make grown-up decisions.

For a moment, his face got even redder, and then his shoulders sagged as he looked at her, anger seeming to fade away as sorrow filled his features.

"Have I been that terrible a father?"

"No, it isn't that, Dad. It's just that Derek and I want to be together. His father is starting a new business, so Derek can leave feeling right about it, and he's going to the city to make something of himself. He will do it, too. He's smart and strong and brings me such joy," she said. Maybe her father would really listen to her for once.

Walking over to her, he leaned down and kissed her cheek. "When did you grow up?" he whispered, making her heart leap.

She had never thought he'd be so willing to accept her decision. She'd thought that she would be leaving the house with him hating her, that it would take years for them to reconcile. She loved Derek enough to risk that, but the thought still saddened her.

"I don't know. Being with Derek is just…just like bees and honey. We fit and he makes me feel grown." What better explanation was there?

"What is this business his father is attempting? Maybe I can help in some way."

In her excitement to earn her father's approval, she never once thought he could be up to no good. This was her dad — the man who had raised her.

"I'm not sure exactly. It's a computer store, I think."

"I will speak to the bank, make sure the loan goes through for his new business."

"You'll do that, Dad?" How could she ever have thought her father cold or uncaring?

"There isn't anything I won't do to make you happy,

princess," he assured her.

They spoke long into the night. She told her father everything, how she and Derek would meet at the church — all of it. Her dad kissed her goodnight and she fell asleep while still planning the future.

That night she called Derek and told him she had a surprise for him, that he would find out at the church when they met. He tried to get her to talk about it, but her dad had told her it would be more meaningful if she did it in person on the day they started their new life.

Because she now had her dad's permission, she thought it a little silly to meet at the church instead of just having him pick her up, but in her romantic heart, it was what she wanted to do, and her father agreed. The church signified the start of a new life.

She anticipated the surprise on Derek's face, and the joy that would flow through him.

Two days later, Jasmine had her bags packed and went in to tell her father goodbye. He hadn't always been the best father, but he had still raised her all on his own, and her eyes filled with tears as she approached him.

"It's time, Dad," she whispered, amazed by how much it hurt to leave. The ecstasy of being with Derek forever outweighed the pain, though. And now there wouldn't be any estrangement; her father was supporting her all the way.

"I can't believe you are moving to the city. Just remember your promise. You won't get married without me there." David was all smiles as he spoke to his daughter.

"I am so happy you want to be there," she said, throwing

her arms around his neck.

"I couldn't miss my baby girl's wedding. Before you go meet Derek, can you do me a favor first? I have an important package that needs to be signed for and I have to run to City Hall for a meeting. Would you wait for it before you go?"

Derek didn't have a cell phone, and she couldn't reach him at his house, but he would be fine if she ran a little late. He knew from experience that she wasn't always punctual, and he'd understand. This was a last request from her dad, and they were parting on good terms.

"Of course, Dad. When will the package arrive?"

"It shouldn't be more than an hour," he promised before kissing her cheek again and then heading out the door.

It was two hours. Jasmine rushed out the door, and made her way to the church fueled by excitement. She carried only a backpack and a small suitcase filled with items she'd need the most. Her father said he'd send the rest when they reached their destination. Fueled by young love and needing nothing more, she was off.

She couldn't believe how good her father was being about all of this.

Derek wasn't there when she arrived, but Jasmine wasn't worried. He'd probably gotten held up, just as she had. Sitting down on the broken church steps, she looked out at the surrounding woods, listening to the sounds of birds chirping, and squirrels scampering through the tree branches.

When an hour passed, she began to grow concerned. Derek was always on time, and this was a big day for the two of them. Wouldn't he send one of his cousins if he were going to be this late? She couldn't imagine that he'd have come and gone. He would have waited, knowing she had been held up since that had often happened while they were dating.

When the sun started to set, she didn't even notice the tears tracking down her face. Maybe he'd changed his mind. Why? What could have possibly made him do such a thing?

She finally accepted he wasn't coming and dragged herself home, crying the entire way. When she walked into the house and her father saw her, he took her into his arms, cradling her the way he'd done when she was a small child.

"What's wrong, Jasmine?" His voice was full of concern.

"He wasn't there. I don't understand," she said between sobs.

"Oh, sweetie, this is what I was worried about," he cooed, making her cry all that much harder.

When she couldn't cry anymore, she made her way to her room and lay alone on her bed, clutching the one picture she had of Derek and her to her heart. Something had to be wrong. He wouldn't have left her there without a valid reason.

Working up the courage to call, she sat with the phone in her hand for almost an hour. Finally, she dialed his house and sat there, holding her breath, as it rang on the other end.

"Hello?" It was Derek. He was home!

She began to smile. Something had come up. It wasn't that he'd left without her.

"Derek?" she barely whispered. Her throat was raw from all the tears she'd shed.

"I have nothing to say to you," he growled into the phone.

"I…I don't understand," she choked out. Never before had

she heard him sound so cruel. His voice was nearly devoid of emotion, just an icy chill running through the line of the telephone.

"You and your father are scum. You'll one day reap what you sow."

The call disconnected and Jasmine stared at the phone for what must have been forever.

"Jasmine?" She looked up to find her dad in the doorway.

"I…What… He sounded so horrible," she said, looking at her dad for answers.

"You shouldn't have called. He made his decision when he left you waiting for him. I never trusted the boy. That's why I had wanted to keep you apart, and I shouldn't have relented, shouldn't have hoped that he was different. Boys like him want one thing, and once they get it, they throw the girls away like they are nothing more than trash. You are better off without him, Jasmine. You'll come to see that soon. We'll just move forward now."

Jasmine lay back down as her father shut the door. Maybe he was right. Maybe Derek had gotten all he'd wanted and he was now done. Sobbing until exhaustion pulled her under, Jasmine felt she'd lost her innocence that night. Her days of being a trusting teenage girl were gone forever.

CHAPTER FOUR

DEREK SAT BACK at his desk, a Cheshire Cat grin dominating his face. The papers were all signed, and now he was the owner of Freeman Industries. He had taken it right out from under David without the bastard having any idea of what was going on. Bad management had left the stocks cheap and easy to buy up.

Though David knew his company was in trouble, the hostile takeover had to have blindsided him. Derek couldn't help but gloat that David had walked into his former offices today only to be met by Derek's security.

Oh, yes, Derek had been tempted to be there, to be sitting in the man's *former* chair, just to see his reaction. He'd barely been able to stop himself, but he had plenty of time to wallow in his victory. He turned around and stared out the huge windows of his office at Titan Industries, looking down at the thriving city of Seattle. Acquiring a new company always gave him a sense of pride, but this one was special. It was the pinnacle of everything he'd been working for over the past ten years.

Derek heard a commotion outside his office and turned around to find that the man in question had barged in through his doorway. *Speak of the devil.*

Derek's secretary came chasing after him. "Sir, you can't go in there," she was gasping out, her voice and eyes panicked.

"It's OK, Lana. I can handle this," he told her.

She apologized and stood there, not knowing what to do.

"You can call security. I have a feeling Mr. Freeman will need to be escorted from the building once we are done talking." The smile never left Derek's face. This confrontation was coming far sooner than he'd expected, and he was enjoying it thoroughly.

"You worthless piece of shit!" David yelled.

"It's good to see you again, David," Derek said, not losing an atom of his cool.

"I was getting things straightened out, and then you swoop in and steal my company out from under me," the man continued to yell.

He was so angry, his face had become completely red, and his voice shook, along with the rest of him. The angrier David got, the calmer Derek felt.

"I guess you should have run your business a bit more lawfully and not left it vulnerable to a takeover," Derek said.

David looked murderous, intent on strangling him if he could make a dash across the room. Derek looked him over with a satisfied contempt. When he was still a teenager, Jasmine's father had seemed larger than life, but he now looked shrunken and old before his time. No threat at all.

"I ran my business successfully for over forty years, you

pompous piece of trash. You may have the rest of the world fooled, but I know where you come from, and I know who you really are," David spat.

Finally, small cracks appeared in Derek's calm. He narrowed his eyes. But he refused to give the man who'd changed his life ten years earlier the reaction he was obviously angling for.

"Unlike you, David, I kept a watchful eye over my business. I may have grown up on the wrong side of town, as you've always liked to point out, but I made choices to change my life. I started with nothing; you're the one who will end up with nothing." Derek's smile mocked the adversary he'd thoroughly bested.

David lunged at him just as the security guards entered the room. Derek held his hand up to stop them from grabbing the man. He wanted David to try to throw a punch. Derek was normally not a violent man, but it would be a total joy to knock David across his pathetic jaw.

David saw the look in Derek's eyes and quickly backed down. "This isn't the last you'll hear from me."

"Security, please escort Mr. Freeman from my building. Let the front desk know he's no longer welcome on the premises." Derek then turned his back on him.

"I'll get you for this; just you wait," David shouted as he was dragged away.

Derek sat down and once again looked over the papers that gave him ownership over Freeman Corporation, with a satisfied smile. He pressed his buzzer. "Lana, would you please pull up those financial documents?"

She brought the material to him, and he got to work.

He hadn't done his usual homework when acquiring the corporation. Before he took a business over, he normally knew it inside and out. He simply hadn't cared with this one — he was buying it up no matter what lay beneath the surface. He didn't even care if the buy ended up costing him millions. He had money to spare. This was about his pride, and nothing more. This was payback.

As he studied the papers over the afternoon, he was surprised to find there were some legitimate reasons to keep the company as it was instead of splitting it up and selling it off, as he'd expected to do. If David had run things the way he should have, the corporation would never have been in jeopardy of a takeover. The man was more of an idiot than Derek had originally thought.

He'd have to think about what he was going to do with this one. If he decided to leave it intact, the first thing to go would be the name. Derek refused to leave that miserable man's name attached to any aspect of the business. If he kept it, it would become *Titan* Medical.

The corporation was a major producer of medical equipment. The product was of high quality, but the marketing department was an abject failure. If the right people were brought in, the company might be worth keeping together.

As he studied through the financial files over the next several days, he discovered that David had apparently embezzled millions of dollars — another of the reasons the company was in such a weak state. He'd leave the legal department to look further into it. No, he wouldn't mind one bit if the man ended up in prison. It would just be icing on the cake.

The minute David had the corporation go public, he had investors to be accountable to. Since David had been stealing from those investors for years, they were going to want answers. Derek's smile grew even wider as he thought about David's life continuing to go down the drain. No, he hadn't always been such a brutal businessman, and he should have felt some shame now at his unholy delight. But he didn't, not in this moment of triumph.

David and Jasmine had ruined his father's chances of getting his own life back on track. They'd stolen his business from him, and they'd be victims of payback for some time to come. They were definitely reaping what they'd sowed so many years earlier.

He decided to keep the current staff for now, but he had memos sent out notifying them that they were going to have to defend their jobs. He normally left all of that for his staff to sort through, but since he was taking this operation personally, he'd decided to conduct a number of the interviews himself.

As Derek prepared to head to the former Freeman Corporation offices with a couple of trusted associates, he was filled with pride. Although he'd made the decision to keep the company essentially as it was, there would be a lot of people losing their jobs and a lot of new hires. It would take months to get everything straightened out.

Time made no difference to him.

As he walked from his office to catch the elevators, his dad approached. "Where are you off to, son?"

"I'm going over to the new company today. I have to eliminate some staff and get the HR set up to hire new employees," Derek said.

"I'll come with you." Daniel climbed in the elevator with him.

"That would be great. I could use an extra person, one I trust, and you're an excellent judge of character," Derek told his dad. He knew his father had a soft heart, but he was also a shrewd businessman.

"Son, I know this has been your dream since that low-life dirtbag hurt you, hurt all of us, but you need to remember that most of these employees didn't even know David Freeman. They're just like you and me, trying to make a living," his father said.

"I hate it when you're right, but I know. Most of the people in executive positions will be replaced, of course. I simply can't trust anyone who worked closely with David. I'm not worried about any of the factory workers. My staff will make sure all of their background checks pass muster, but other than that, I'll leave them alone — well, not entirely," he added.

"What do you mean?" his dad asked.

"David was underpaying the factory workers while padding the executives' pockets. They are barely making minimum wage." Derek almost sputtered. "I'm going to raise their pay and offer bonuses for high work production and early completion of projects."

"That's why you're so successful, son. You actually care about the core of the company," his father told him.

Derek knew what it was like barely to be able to survive, and he followed the Golden Rule when it came to his employees. And so his turnover rate was low — once people came to work for him, they didn't leave.

"The bastard didn't even offer health insurance for his factory workers. It really is no wonder he lost everything," Derek continued to rage.

"Well, just remember that these people are scared about their jobs and don't know that you're different. It would be a good idea if the first thing you do is call a meeting and reassure them," Daniel said.

"You're right again, Dad. I wasn't planning on doing that personally, but I'll call a meeting first thing tomorrow. But, I want to spend today looking around and then eliminating some of the deadweight."

"Sounds like a plan, son." Daniel slapped Derek on the back.

A FEW DAYS later, Derek rode to the new office building in silence. He was immensely satisfied to see the crew working on the new sign out front. *Titan Medical* was on its way up. He couldn't wait for it to be unveiled.

Derek walked into the building surrounded by his best team members and his father. He knew they made an intimidating sight, but he did his best to make eye contact and not frighten the regular staff. They were just trying to make a living, and none of them knew what David had been up to for years.

His team approached building security. That had been the first change he'd made. He always put in his own security team immediately.

"Good morning, Mr. Titan. It's good to see you," the guard said.

"Hello, Tim. How are things going here?"

"Everything has been mellow the last few days. Mr. Freeman tried to come in the day after the takeover, but he was escorted out and hasn't been back since," the man reported.

"I've had new badges created, and no one will enter without one after today. All employees who are kept on will receive a badge before they leave work. There will be a lot of people let go, and I don't need them sneaking back in and causing trouble. I also want several security personnel up on the twenty-fifth floor to escort people down as soon as they're let go. Today, unfortunately, isn't going to be a pleasant one."

"No problem, Mr. Titan. I'll send them up right away," he answered.

"Here's your new badge and some for your men. Crews will be here over the next few days setting up keypads for all the elevators and exits. Here's the list of people who will be doing the work. These people, and only these people, are allowed in. If their company tries to send over replacements, call me and I'll let you know if they're approved or not," he finished.

"OK, boss," Tim replied, and then set to work making phone calls.

Derek spent the first part of the morning exploring the huge building in more detail than he'd managed to do the other day. Most of his time was spent down on the bottom floors, assessing the factory and its workers. They were eyeing him with trepidation, and he knew his father was right. He needed to speak with them soon. The work was going slowly, and he saw obvious mistakes being made. He knew that part of the reason had to do with their lack of enthusiasm for underpaid work, and part was because that they were so unsure of their futures.

He decided to call a meeting right away.

He spoke to his men, who went in search of the foreman or forewoman on each floor. In only half an hour, he had all the factory workers assembled. He looked out at about five hundred apprehensive faces. Even in Seattle, the job market for workers with their skills was in the dumps, and everyone was afraid of helping to swell the ranks of the unemployed.

He stood at the makeshift lectern and grabbed the microphone. "You all look worried, so I'll cut to the chase. My name is Derek Titan, and I'm the new owner of this corporation. First, I want to assure you all that we plan to keep this business up and running." He could hear a whooshing sound as many in the audience breathed out a sigh of relief.

"There will be some changes made, but I think you'll like what we have in mind. It will benefit every one of you. I've looked through the financial records, and you've been woefully underpaid and not offered any benefits. You'll receive a ten percent wage increase, and health insurance will be provided. By the end of the day, you'll receive paperwork showing the changes. You'll have to go through a background check to continue working here, but you'll see that the working environment is going to be much better from here on out."

He now saw smiles in front of him, and some mouths gaped open. He had to fight his own smile from spreading across his face. He needed to appear confident and in charge. He couldn't appear to be a friend — the boss had to be respected, not necessarily liked — but these people deserved a lot better than they'd had under David.

"If you work hard for me and meet production deadlines, you'll be rewarded. I want to turn this company around into what it should be. You make high-quality products here, so let's be a high-quality company as well. I want investors to walk through these stations and see happy employees doing a top-quality job. The better you do, the more bonuses you'll get. We'll be setting up some HR representatives down here and bringing each of you in over the next few days to sign paperwork. This is a new corporation, and if you do choose to leave, we'll offer you a severance package. If you have any questions, please wait until you're called in so we can move things along quickly Anyway, please return to work, and your bosses will be calling you in over the next few days. I need all the supervisors to meet me over here, please," he concluded.

He explained to the supervisors what they'd be doing in more detail, made sure the employees staying would be cleared for their new badges, and then made his way up to the executive offices for the first time since the takeover. A few secretaries glanced warily at him as he passed, but not many other people were around.

He walked up to David Freeman's old office and sighed. As he stepped through the doorway, he felt an overwhelming sense of accomplishment. The furniture had already been replaced. He hadn't wanted to sit in the same seat or use the same desk as that man. He hadn't touched the other offices, but this one would be his when he was working there, and it needed to suit him and the way he worked. And that wasn't at all the way David Freeman had worked.

He sat down in his chair and turned it toward the large windows. The space wasn't as nice as the one back at his main office, but it would do. There were brand-new cherry wood floors and comfortable but elegant furniture. Priceless pieces of art hung on the walls and a top-of-the-line computer system had been installed. He knew it showed weakness, but because of his beginnings in poverty, he liked surrounding himself with the finer things in life. And who would dare to say anything about it to him?

The view from the huge windows gave him a few minutes of peace before he had to continue his day. It was going to be a very long one, and he'd be lucky to get out of there before midnight. People were never happy to be fired, and he had a lot of people to let go.

He sighed as he turned back to the computer and started looking through the personnel files. It was time to learn who currently occupied the new offices at Titan Medical.

CHAPTER FIVE

JASMINE HAD TO fight back tears as she walked into the familiar building. There were men outside working on placing a new sign. It was more proof that the company no longer belonged to her father. She'd been trying to reach him for days to ask him what had happened, but without luck. He hadn't even told her the company was in any jeopardy of being taken over, and now this.

Her dad wasn't answering his phone or returning her calls. She'd been to his house several times and was told he wasn't there. That morning, when she tried again, she wasn't able to get past the gates and saw a real estate sign on his front lawn.

Yes, she understood what a hostile takeover was, but she didn't understand how it had happened to her father, didn't know why this was going on. She really didn't get why he was suddenly refusing to speak to her.

Their relationship was far from good, to put it lightly, but this was a big deal and she would have thought that he'd at least have let her know if she needed to look for new work.

Didn't she deserve that much respect?

All she knew at this moment was that the new owner of Freeman Corporation was scheduled to be there today, and she was determined to get some answers. Jasmine wasn't overly fond of her job, but it paid the bills — barely — and she needed to know whether her position was secure. She didn't hold out much hope, though.

She'd read about the hostile takeover on the first day, and then she'd refused to open another newspaper. She wanted to get firsthand knowledge, whether it was from her father or from the new owner. So here she was.

As she passed through the doors over which new workers were hanging a covered sign, her frustration deflated. Just seeing her father's name removed brought home that all of this was real.

If she'd had only herself to think about, she'd probably just walk out. As the owner's daughter, she didn't stand much of a chance at keeping her position, after all. Still, the new owner might not know who she was, and she was desperate enough to fight for her job if he didn't. That was cowardice on her part, but she needed the paycheck. Any paycheck.

She hadn't wanted to have people think she hadn't earned her position on her own merits, so she'd chosen to use her mother's maiden name instead of using Freeman. Would that save her job now?

She trembled when she thought about her beautiful son, who was at home waiting for her. He was the reason she had to fight like hell to stay here. He looked so much like his father, it made her heart ache sometimes, but his character was so different than Derek's.

Her son had integrity and honor. He was beautiful inside and out. Nothing should make her think of Derek with anything other than contempt, but sometimes it was so hard when she looked into her son's eyes. Still, why in the world did she ever miss Derek? She had to remind herself that her son's father wasn't who she'd believed he was when she'd been a naïve teen.

She started to pass the security desk, but she was stopped. "Sorry, Ms. Sanders, but we have a new procedure now. Can you step over here?" the guard asked.

"What's going on, here?" she asked, perplexed.

"A new security system, starting today," Tim told her. He looked through his computer screen until he found her name. He typed in some information and then handed her a new badge. "This is just a temporary one. The boss is doing a bunch of cuts, and when everything is done, the remaining employees will be issued permanent badges." His look was regretful, and she knew that her job was probably doomed.

She got on the elevator and took a fortifying breath. If she was headed for defeat, she was certainly going to go out fighting. This new boss sounded like a real piece of work.

Though her job was tedious, it wasn't all bad. She was proud that she'd hired most of the factory workers, and she was more afraid for them than for anyone else. She'd fought her father many times to give them better wages and benefits, but he had treated her like a child, telling her she didn't know how to run a successful business.

That was a bit ironic now; look where all his business savvy had gotten him. Why wouldn't he talk to her and explain what was going on?

Jasmine walked into her office to find several strangers looking through her computer files. "What is going on in here?" she demanded.

"Who are you?" an extremely attractive blonde asked her in a clipped voice.

"I happen to be the Human Resources director, and this is my office you're rifling through. Who the heck are you?" she replied.

"I'm Amy Snailer, and *we're* the current HR team. We're working on who will be staying or going. The owner asked us to escort you to his office as soon as you returned," the woman said coolly.

"It would be my pleasure to see the man." Jasmine turned on her heels. She'd give the man a piece of her mind. It was rude to have people going through her files without consulting her first. She figured she was getting fired, anyway, so she'd say what she wanted to.

She knew the floor well and stormed toward her father's old office, figuring the man would choose it for his own. After all, it was the largest in the building, and the guy seemed to be power mad. Amy was running behind her, trying to catch up.

Stalking past the surprised secretary, Jasmine didn't even bother knocking. She threw open the door and strode toward the desk. The man was sitting with his back to her, but she didn't care. He'd hear her just fine no matter which way he was facing.

"Who the hell do you think you are, sending a bunch of

strangers into my office to go through my files? I would have been more than happy to show them anything they'd asked for, but the way you're running things here is a complete invasion of privacy, both mine and that of the employees here," she almost shouted. She rarely raised her voice, but she was so angry, she couldn't control herself.

"I'm so sorry, Mr. Titan. She returned from lunch and then stormed out of the HR offices before I could stop her," Amy almost gasped. Jasmine's whole world seemed to come to a standstill as the woman said his name. He turned slowly in his chair, and their eyes connected.

She couldn't breathe as she realized that the man who had turned her world upside down again was none other than the cad who had taken her virginity and left her without a word.

She'd known Derek had made a name for himself, knew he was some international big shot, but she'd had no clue he was back in Seattle, back so close to her…and to their son. Did he know she worked here? Was he playing a sick game? Why? Nothing seemed to make sense.

Her knees would no longer hold her up, and she sank down into a chair that was luckily right behind her. The seconds ticked by as they stared at each other.

"Thank you, Amy. You can leave us now." That was all he said in his cold, controlled voice.

"But, sir, you said you wanted one of us in here as you let people go…" she protested.

"I said *leave*." Amy looked at him with surprise, but quickly pulled herself together and left the room, but not before slipping Jasmine a challenging look.

Jasmine wouldn't put it past Derek to be sleeping with his employees. He was rich as sin now and apparently thought he could do anything he wanted.

"I didn't realize you worked here. I guess I should have spent more time studying the personnel file," he finally said. He'd figured the princess hadn't worked a day in her life.

"Why would you do this?" she asked. Why would he want to destroy her father? Derek had been the one to walk away. Why would he possibly come back into her life in such a detestable manner? He'd already gotten what he wanted from her.

"It was a good deal," he answered; ice encased his voice and his eyes.

And Jasmine's hackles rose. Where did he get off with such a dismissive attitude? He really was a coldhearted bastard.

They sat staring at each other, and she refused to be the one to break the silence.

"What position do you hold here?" he asked with a smirk, as if he couldn't imagine she'd know how to work. His tone infuriated her even further.

"I'm the head of personnel, and I do an excellent job," she said between clenched teeth. He didn't say anything as he pulled her file up on his computer. He sat there, going through the file for a full ten minutes, while she remained in the chair, fuming.

"Smart. You used another last name. Had I realized, I would have had you in here much sooner. It seems that you have worked here for six years. I'm surprised you bothered going to college." His look at her was derisive.

"I now go by my mother's maiden name. I graduated at the

top of my class, and I'm excellent in my position. If you fire me, I'll sue you for wrongful termination."

"You'll soon find I don't take well to being threatened, Ms. Freeman," he said, refusing to use the name she chose to go by. "I'm not firing you…today, but you'll only remain on the staff for now on a trial basis. Let's call it idle curiosity. However, if you don't work to my far stricter standards, then you'll be let go." He leaned back in his chair.

She wanted to stand up and slap him across his smug face. She had never in her life been so angry. How could he look at her so coldly? How could he have turned into such a cruel, heartless man? She was grateful he'd left her before she knew she was pregnant, grateful he didn't know about their son — she was sure he would have tried to acquire him the same way he acquired his businesses.

"I do my job very well. I expect to be treated like any other employee here. I also don't want to speak with you anymore," she said as she stood up to leave. She needed to find a bathroom quickly, where she could break down in private.

Before she'd taken more than a few steps, he grabbed her arm, and she was suddenly standing far too close to him. She cursed the way her traitorous body wanted to lean up against him. His smell was invading her senses, making the heat pool up in her core.

No, no, no, she shouted at herself. *This is wrong; this is sick.* She refused to let him affect her. How could she feel anything toward such a tyrant, and worse, toward the man who had broken her heart?

It had been ten years since she'd seen him. Time should

have erased any good memories she had of him.

CHAPTER SIX

I **T WOULD BE** hard to treat you like any other employee, since you're the only one here I've sunk deep inside while you cried out my name," he whispered, bringing his lips only centimeters from her own. "And I hate to tell you this, but as head of personnel you'll be working *very* closely with me; after all, we'll be replacing quite a few positions in this company. If you can't handle the *position*, please feel free to walk out right now," he growled.

Derek's intent was to get to her, but his body was betraying him, dammit. The second he touched her arm, lightning shot through his fingertips, straight to his groin. Her subtle, delicate scent surrounded him. He wanted to haul her into his arms and take her immediately on his new desk.

He was trying to play with her, and instead, *he* was the one who was getting burned. If it hadn't been for her eyes widening in desire, or the fact that her breathing was getting shallow, he would have completely lost it. Seeing that she wasn't immune to him, even now, gave him back some strength. Yes, he would have her again, but it would be on his terms, and *he'd* be the one to walk away and leave her wanting more.

She might look innocent, but he knew how cold the blood was that ran through her veins. He hadn't been good enough for her, but it hadn't been enough for her to just walk away. She'd had to destroy his father's life, too.

He would never be so stupid as to trust her again. His body needed convincing that she was evil, though, because ten years might as well have just evaporated by the way he was reacting to her.

It took every ounce of his control, but he finally stepped back and casually propped himself on the edge of his desk. He hoped, at least, that he looked as if she hadn't affected him at all. Years in business had made him a master at putting on masks, but she was certainly testing him.

She had her hands clenched at her sides while she tried to pull herself together. It was easy to wait her out, easy to mock her with a brutal smile.

"First of all, what happened in the past is long over, Mr. Titan. I hadn't thought about you since the last day we were together. Had you not brought it up, I would have completely forgotten we even had sex," she lied. She felt some pleasure at his quick change in posture. She'd wiped that smile off his face, and she was delighted to see his eyes narrow.

She was happy to go on with her little speech. "Secondly, I can handle anything you throw at me. If we need to work together, I can stand being around you. I just prefer not to."

She made what she deemed a dignified exit.

But as soon as she was out of his office, she raced down

the hallway and into the ladies' room, where she lost her breakfast. She sat huddled on the floor for several minutes as she struggled to regain her composure. How could she possibly handle working for this man? He'd destroyed her completely, and she'd been too afraid to get involved in any other relationships ever since. Except for one, she thought with a tender smile. Her son.

She'd try to work for Derek as long as she could while she started searching for another job, but she couldn't go without a paycheck. She had her son to think about, and since her dad had long ago cut off her trust fund, she lived paycheck to paycheck. Her pay was pitiful considering her position, and she didn't have a lot in the way of savings since she spent every extra penny sending her son to a good private school in the city, with all the academic and recreational trimmings.

After allowing herself a total of about five minutes, she pulled herself together and walked proudly back into her old office. Amy was still there, and though she tried putting on a professional mask, Jasmine wasn't fooled. It was obvious the woman had been hoping she'd seen the last of Jasmine.

"If you would please move, I need to get to my desk," Jasmine said, proud of the authority in her voice.

"He didn't fire you?"

"He has no reason to fire me. I'm excellent at my job." Jasmine was relieved when Amy made a quick exit.

"I need to gather all the files to go over with Mr. Titan. May I please have some privacy?" she asked the two other people in the room. The steel in her voice left no doubt that, although she phrased it as a request, it was a demand. They were to leave immediately. This was still her office, and she wanted it to herself.

They left without a word. Were they running to the boss to find out whether she could kick them out? She simply didn't care.

The day had just started, but it already felt as if it were the longest of her life. How was she going to keep her composure all afternoon, let alone all week? All she could think of were pep talks — something she'd perfected over the past ten years.

So much time had passed since Derek had stood her up virtually at the altar, then ended their relationship for good with a few scathing words over the telephone.

Teenagers got their hearts broken every single day; it wasn't such a big deal, and she was healthy enough to move forward. If she let him affect her now, she was giving him power over her, and that wasn't something she was willing to do. The consequences could be disastrous.

Taking a deep breath and muttering the word *courage* to herself, she turned toward her computer, banishing Derek from her thoughts. He lingered there in the back of her mind, but every time he tried to take over, she pushed him back once again.

She'd fought her entire life to make something of herself, had become a teenage mother, and still managed to get herself through college, all on her own. Her father certainly hadn't been supportive when he'd found out.

His support and kindness the night Derek had left her had ended when she'd come to him for comfort the day she'd taken the pregnancy test.

She'd wanted so many times to call Derek, tell him about the baby. But her pride had kept her from doing that. His entire family — his father and his two cousins —had moved by that time. Since his father's business hadn't worked out, there'd been no reason for them to stay in the small town just outside of Seattle, anymore.

She hadn't heard a word about Derek for several years, and then one day he'd appeared in her local paper.

Local boy makes good with first million-dollar paycheck, the headline had read. She'd rushed from the store and thrown up. Below the headline had been a picture of a slightly older Derek with his arm wrapped around a cheap blonde in a tight dress.

Through the years she'd seen more headlines, more news about the rapidly rising Derek Titan. Her one weakness had been saving the papers that featured only him. That way if ever her son truly begged to see what his father looked like, she could show him.

The issue had come up a few times, but not enough that she'd felt forced to reveal to him who his father was. Still, guilt ate away at her on those occasions that her son was one of the few kids without a dad rooting them on at a baseball game or wrestling match.

That's why Jasmine was always the loudest parent in the crowd. It wasn't enough, but she did what she needed to do because she loved him with all her heart.

Enough. Pushing the depressing thoughts from her mind, she turned back to her computer and got to work. Of course Derek intended to fire her, but she wouldn't go down without a fight.

CHAPTER SEVEN

DEREK SAT BACK down at his desk. He was angry with Jasmine, but he was far angrier with himself. He couldn't believe he'd let her get to him. That was missing the whole point of his revenge.

How delicious to discover that she worked for the company! He'd simply been planning to cut off her supply of easy money by breaking her father. Had he known she was an employee, his plans would have altered a bit. She was smart to use another name — very smart. Ah, things were going so much better than he had hoped. He'd been expecting her to appear at his door, begging him to show her father mercy.

Instead he had her working under him.

Under him.

That thought made his groin tighten once more. He wanted her beneath him again, despite what she'd done. He wouldn't take her, however, until he was more in control of himself. He'd hardly be teaching her a lesson for what she'd done if he fell for her all over again, gave her that power over him. He ran his hand through his hair in frustration — how easily she got to him.

There was a knock at his door, and he looked up in irritation. Where was his secretary? Before he could call out and invite the person to enter, the doorknob turned and Amy appeared. The look in his eye at her boldness didn't seem to faze her.

She walked over to him, not quite able to control the fury in her eyes. "I thought we were going to be discussing everyone in the executive offices who was going to remain on staff or be let go."

She was trying to control her temper, trying to put a sexy and enticing smile on her face, but she was failing miserably. Her constant pursuit of him only increased his foul mood. If she hadn't been such a shark when it came to business and a good addition to his staff, he would have let her go long ago.

"I'm assuming you're talking about Ms. Freeman," he said, not bothering with the name she'd been using on her records. Jasmine was David's daughter, and he needed to remind himself of that fact often.

"Ms. Freeman?" she asked in surprise. "You mean *that woman* is actually Ms. Freeman? Is she related to the previous owner?"

"Yes, she's his daughter, and I'm letting her keep her position for now," he said in a voice that brooked no argument.

Amy gave him a perplexed look while she tried to control her anger. Why was she taking this so personally? It puzzled him.

"Are you keeping her as some sort of power strategy?" she asked hopefully.

"Something like that," he answered nonchalantly. The answer seemed to satisfy her.

She sidled up to him. "Do you want to do lunch? I know it's early still, but I'm starving. Or I could order in. Then we could eat here while discussing more employment strategies." She leaned on the edge of his desk, her short skirt hitching up.

Her flash of thigh was wasted on him; in fact, the only thing he saw clearly was that it was time to let her go. No matter how good she was at her job, this was just too much for him to deal with right now. Up to this point, she'd certainly hinted she wanted more, but hadn't been so bold about it. "Why don't you and the others go out to an early lunch? I have a lot to get done before we start bringing people in. Besides, I'll be going over records with Ms. Freeman soon," Derek told her.

Her eyes narrowed a bit at the mention of Jasmine's name, and it cemented his decision to fire her. He wasn't going to tolerate a jealous woman in his business, especially when she had nothing to be jealous about. Would he ever find a woman who played straight with him? It seemed he wasn't so lucky.

There was another knock on the door, and then his two most trusted employees stepped in, looking a bit frazzled. "What is it?" he asked. They weren't easily shaken.

"We just got kicked out of the HR office, and we weren't sure of what you wanted us to do, so we thought it smarter to talk to you than to cause a scene," Greg said.

"I see. Well, you did the right thing. Ms. Freeman and I will be talking, but for now, go have lunch, and we'll get it all worked out this afternoon," Derek said. His employees' eyes widened a bit at her name, but they quickly turned, rushing from the room instead of saying anything.

He needed a break. It was always difficult when you had to fire people, especially when the takeover was a complete surprise to all those involved. He never enjoyed this part of his job, not even in this building, he was finding. Still, the employees in this company who were getting the boot would certainly deserve it. And then there was Amy...

The two men left before he could change his mind. Amy lingered for a moment longer and then followed them out the door.

He called his head office and spoke to personnel there. He had them arrange a severance package for Amy and would have her employment ended before the day was out. Once she got back from lunch, he'd send her over to corporate headquarters.

Dismissing Amy from his mind, he got busy with his work, before ordering food to be delivered and then walking over to Jasmine's office. He stood at her door and watched her for several minutes without her noticing him. When she finally looked up and their eyes collided, he felt as if he were being punched in the gut again.

When was that feeling going to end?

He was sure it was simply because it had been so long since he'd seen her last. The anticipation of what was to come was obviously the cause of his out-of-control hormones.

"Have you gathered together the files?" he asked, proud of the chill in his voice.

"Yes, everything is together, but it would be easier to do it here. There's a lot, and it will take several trips to get them to your office," she said. "I really don't understand why you don't want to use the computer."

"I like to have the physical papers to look at. It gets old staring at a computer screen all day. Besides, I prefer my office. We have a large table where we can spread everything out. Also, that's where we'll be calling people in, so it's more convenient," he said. He didn't know why he was bothering to explain himself. Her job was to do what he told her, no questions asked.

She blew her breath out in frustration before standing up. "Fine, we can do it your way, but I'm not breaking my back to lug all these boxes over there," she said and strode regally out the door.

Before Derek could stop himself, he felt a smile tug across his features. She was definitely hot when she was angry, and she'd been angry ever since she'd first walked into his office. He was now looking forward to the lengthy afternoon.

Derek commandeered several of the security guards to transport the boxes to his office. By the time they got everything over, lunch had arrived. He'd ordered a good selection of salads and sandwiches and offered some to Jasmine, but she refused. He smiled at her stubbornness.

"Can we please get started? I can't stay late tonight."

He was instantly irritated again. It was time to put her in her place. She was no longer the daughter of the boss, and she needed to understand that right away.

"You need to realize that during a restructuring of a company this size, there will be many nights of overtime. I expect you to put in the hours needed to make this place a success if you expect to keep your job," he told her.

Her shoulders slumped, and he was surprised to not feel joy at her defeat. He couldn't figure out what was wrong with him. He wanted to destroy her, so why was his little victory not pounding through his veins?

She pulled out the first file, and they went through it. He'd started to make two different piles on the table. One was a stack with records of the employees who had no chance of keeping their jobs. The other was a stack of files for employees who would at least get the opportunity to interview with him. If he liked what they had to say, they'd keep their position. If not, curtains.

When Amy returned with the others, he sent her to the main offices. He didn't miss the look she shot at Jasmine as she went out the door, reinforcing his decision to let her go.

He sent his men into the conference room next door with a few files so they could start calling in employees to be let go. And it wasn't long before he could hear shouting through his walls.

Derek was used to the process, having gone through it multiple times before. But he could see Jasmine tensing beside him, her eyes straying to the open door as people stormed by.

Although she didn't say anything, it was obvious that she'd rather be just about anywhere else. Her resolve was stronger than he'd initially given her credit for.

The afternoon continued and it wasn't until six in the evening when Jasmine looked up wearily. "I really need to get home. I have something I have to do tonight," she said.

His eyes narrowed to dangerous slits. Was she late for a date? He knew it was none of his business, but he'd decided he wanted her in his bed again, and he didn't want another man interfering.

"We can work on this more tomorrow. I can already see it will take us all week," he said, not letting her know how much he wanted to question her. No problem. He'd just have to find an excuse to go to her place within the next couple of days to find out why she was in such a hurry to leave.

"Thank you," she muttered, as if it were choking her to say the words, and then she scrambled to her feet as if she couldn't get away fast enough.

After she was safely from his sight, Derek stood up and gathered his own belongings together. There was no reason for him to stay any later that night.

He walked from the nearly empty building and drove home alone. There was a slight spring in his step as he opened the door to his house. Sparring with Jasmine had been surprisingly stimulating, elevating his mood. Wiping the smile from his lips, he reminded himself that this was nothing more than revenge.

It might just take a few glasses of scotch before he believed his own thoughts.

CHAPTER EIGHT

JASMINE RUSHED THROUGH the door of the school gym. She hadn't even had time to run home and change. Her son was in the fourth grade and was very proud to be on the wrestling team. He had a meet that started twenty minutes ago, and she was praying she hadn't missed his match.

Nearly skidding to a stop, she was moving so quickly, relief filled her when she found where the children were sitting. It didn't seem that he'd had his match yet. She wanted to give Jacob a kiss, but she knew that would embarrass him in front of all his friends, so she took a breath and slowed her pace as she approached.

"I didn't miss your match, did I?" she asked.

"No, Mom, I'm up next," he said with a shrug. Jacob was trying to act as if it didn't matter, but she could see the relief in his eyes. There hadn't been a single game or event of his that she had missed, and it pleased her to know that her presence mattered to him.

"Good. I'm sorry I got here so late, but there was some

extra work to be done at the office."

"It's OK, Mom," he told her in his far-too-understanding voice, making her smile.

After a quick ruffle of his hair, she walked over to the bleachers and sat down. When it was her son's turn on the floor, she cheered him on and clapped the loudest in the crowd when he won — well, of course she did. It was her son, after all.

He ran up to her and gave her a rare public hug afterward, forgetting for a minute he was too old to show his mother open affection.

"I'm so proud of you," she had to say.

"Thanks, Mom. I have to go back over with the team now." He practically danced back over toward his teammates, who high-fived him as he entered their circle.

She heartily wished she could go back to being a child, carefree and so easily excited, so easily happy.

That thought made her stomach clench. She remembered the excitement that had rushed through her body when Derek stood so close earlier that day. She should feel nothing but loathing, but one afternoon in his presence left her only more confused.

Stop, she told herself. She was with her son now and wouldn't think of Derek. She had to put up with him at the office, but he wasn't allowed to invade her private time. She sighed as she realized how hard it was going to be when she had to work with him all day.

Age had been far too good to him. His boyish muscles had matured, and when he'd taken off his suit jacket, exposing his wide shoulders and large biceps, she'd had to fight to keep from drooling. She'd once known his body as intimately as humanly possible, and she missed the feel of his hands on her. She hadn't felt the touch of any man in far too long. Not since her last night with Derek. The only man whose touch she'd felt.

Maybe it was time to start dating again. Jacob's wrestling coach had asked her out, and though she'd put him off, perhaps she should just accept the invitation. Best to think about it first, though; action was dangerous with her hormones in such an uproar.

When the meet was over and Jacob had helped his team put the equipment away, he met his mom at the bleachers.

"What sounds good for dinner?" Jasmine asked, tempted to take his backpack, but standing down to let her little man do it himself. It was hard to let him grow up.

"I don't know," he mumbled, fiddling with the straps on his bag.

"Hmm, how about frog toes and bug juice, then?" she asked with a straight face.

"You're so gross, Mom," he gasped, but she got a laugh from him.

"Yeah, I never did like frog — too salty. How about liver and onions?"

"Fine. You win!" He scrunched his forehead while thinking it all over. "Can we get pizza and take it home? I want to play catch before the sun goes down."

"Pizza and catch it is," she said.

The two of them swung by the pizza parlor in her minivan and picked up his favorite, pepperoni with extra cheese, and then played catch for an hour.

As it got closer to bedtime, Jasmine felt her throat aching with the need to talk to Jacob about Derek, but she'd kept her secret for so long that she didn't know how to open this door. She'd never spoken badly about Derek, but she also hadn't told him who his father was.

When she tucked Jacob in that night, she could feel the words on the tip of her tongue, but this wasn't the right time. She would confess all to her son — just not yet.

The next morning, Jasmine tried to ignore the butterflies in her stomach as she rode the elevator up to her floor. She was hoping Derek would have other things to do in his home office; she didn't know how many days in a row she could stand being with him from sunup to sundown before she fell apart and confessed everything.

Besides the secret she carried, why did he have to smell so good? It was messing with her head and he was a stuffy executive, for goodness' sake. When she was in the same room with him, she couldn't banish from her head the old images of herself wrapped in his arms. It was a struggle, but she kept reminding herself that not only had he walked away from her after stealing her innocence, but he'd then compounded the crime by coming back to take over her father's company.

It would do her well to remember how heartless he was.

She couldn't slip and tell him about their son. He cared only for himself, and anything he deemed his, he took mercilessly. She refused to lose Jacob to him — the boy was her entire world.

No more than five minutes after she sat down at her desk, her phone buzzed, and she knew who was on the line.

"When did you get in? I've been trying to reach you for an hour," Derek snapped over the line.

"I got here a few minutes ago, and I'm twenty minutes early as it is," she said with frustration.

"Get over here. We have a lot more work to do." Having issued his command, he hung up.

She took a calming breath — no need to antagonize him by telling him precisely what she thought about his waspish tone — and then she sat there in her office for a few minutes just to let him stew and also to prove she was her own person. Yes, he was her boss for now, but that didn't give him the right to behave like a barbarian.

Did he treat his other employees this way? Or was it only those he'd slept with and then turned his back on? OK, maybe she was being a bit overdramatic, but he was being an ass, and she was stressed out enough as it was.

When she finally felt calm enough to head to his office, her phone began buzzing again. She ignored it. Gosh, he was impatient!

After shutting her door behind her with a sigh, she walked wearily to his office. The secretary wasn't even there, and she passed a raft of empty offices along the way. He really was changing everything about the building. She didn't particularly like any of the people who were getting fired, but it was still comforting to have familiar faces around her. And he was taking even that away.

She took one more fortifying breath before she turned the knob on his door and stepped through, her eyes locking with his in a tense showdown as he held the phone to his ear.

Carefully sitting the handset down, he looked at her grimly, and the only thought going through Jasmine's head was *bring it on.*

CHAPTER NINE

DEREK FORCED HIS features to betray nothing when Jasmine walked in. She was wearing a green skirt suit with dark trim that matched her bewitching eyes to perfection and intensified their effect, and though she had her hair up in an unflattering bun *again* — he really wanted to take it down — it still didn't detract from the sublime beauty of her face. She wore hardly any makeup, but she was one of the few women who simply didn't need it.

The challenge in her eyes was like throwing a red scarf in front of a bull. He wanted to accept and then charge. He fought to remain seated as she moved closer.

Though she was trying to play it cool, he could see the nerves jumping beneath her skin, see the worry in her eyes. Yes, he was affecting her as much as she was affecting him. His desire was by no means one-sided, and he had valid reasons for his part of the equation.

Deep down he knew he was feeding himself a line, but he pushed that unwanted thought aside.

Jasmine sat at the table, and after a few silent moments, he joined her. Her light scent drifted over to him, and he could feel his pulse start to race and his lower anatomy wake up. He'd have to take her much sooner than he'd originally planned just to dislodge her from his system. Then he could get his libido back in check.

At least her breathing had deepened as he joined her, and her chest was rapidly rising and falling. He could even see her pulse speed up through the delicate skin of her neck.

Knowing he was a fool, but unable to resist, he decided to test the very limits of his control.

He scooted his chair closer to her than was needed or appropriate. She obviously wanted to move away, but she was apparently too stubborn to show any weakness in front of him. Their shoulders brushed together as he leaned in to look at the file she had just opened in front of her.

"So, what have you been doing the last ten years?" he asked out of the blue. For once in his life he had not an ounce of interest in the business at hand. Learning everything about her was at the forefront.

"That's none of your business. It has nothing to do with my job," she snapped, and she tried to pull his attention back to the file. "This is Anthony. He works in accounting. I have spoken to him on a few occasions and even went to my father because some of his business practices appeared unethical, but my father said nothing was going on. I would personally not trust him, or have him work for me." She pushed the folder closer to him.

Bringing up her father was as good as throwing cold water

in his face — and onto his lap. That was a libido killer. He looked through the exceptionally detailed folder and then added Anthony to the "fire" pile. Jasmine immediately picked up another folder.

Small talk was forgotten as they continued to go through the files, one by one, and for the most part, the two of them agreed on who deserved a chance to stay, but every once in a while they clashed heatedly.

But when she argued for someone to stay on, she lost. Once he'd set his mind on something, it was difficult to change it. Nearly impossible, actually.

Her hopes weren't high when they fought over yet another employee. She'd brought forward the file and made her case for continuing to employ the man, but Derek had decided to let him go. Yet when he tossed the file into the termination pile, she determinedly snatched it back out.

"I *really* think you need to interview Henry. He's a good man and does exceptional work. You don't even know him, so you can give him the courtesy of at least speaking with him before you end his employment," she demanded.

Derek raised his eyes at her outburst. She'd argued for a few people, but she certainly hadn't been so emphatic about it. So he really had to wonder who this Henry was and if he was possibly her reason for having to leave yesterday. Derek moved the man's file over to the interview pile just to see who his competition was.

"Thank you," she said, although it came out through clenched teeth and didn't sound like a thank-you at all. It sounded as if she wanted to call him a few choice names.

"I need lunch. Let's go out," he said as the office was starting to close in on him.

"I'll eat in," she replied.

"It will be a business lunch, so you'll accompany me." He grabbed his jacket and walked to the door, holding it open for her. The smile he threw her was a challenge, a clear attempt to see her next move.

After a tense moment, she got up stiffly and followed him from the room. He could practically see the steam rising from her ears. His amusement at her attitude surprised him — he wasn't used to being disobeyed so openly, but he liked that she was unafraid to challenge him.

As the two of them stepped into the elevator and he pushed the lobby button, he turned to face her, not quite sure what he was going to say next. The mystery of it all appealed to him.

"If you keep clenching your teeth like that, you will end up having jaw troubles," he told her.

Jasmine looked at him incredulously for a moment before she unlocked her jaw and turned her lips up in a grimace of a smile.

"Is this better, Derek? Should I bow or curtsy too? Is there anything else that I'm doing wrong?" she asked in a voice of honey dripping with venom.

"Well, since you asked…" he started.

The look she sent him should have melted him to the metal walls of the elevator. It certainly wasn't a ladylike smile. Derek suddenly found himself resisting a chuckle as her cheeks glowed in her temper.

"I want this job, I really do, but I swear to you that if you dare answer one of those questions, I won't be held accountable for my response," she said, her voice shaking with her fierce struggle to control the rage.

"Then why ask?" he countered.

"Don't try to act stupid. We both know how very smart you are. I was the fool to believe all your pack of lies," she snapped, a sudden shine washing over her eyes.

She turned quickly away and when she looked back, her face was under control; had he imagined her vulnerable look? Either way, he was beginning to feel like a heel. He didn't like it — she was the one who should be feeling that way. She and her father had cost him so much — had cost his family so much.

Doubt filled him, though. Drew thought she'd been innocent, that what had happened was all her father's doing. But that made no sense; she had betrayed his family to her father. Still, his cousin had tried numerous times to have him speak with her. Why should he have bothered? Anyway, he'd been so filled with rage and hurt that he was afraid of what he'd do or say, so he'd shut his cousin off. He'd vowed she wasn't going to get away with her action, but he'd needed time to exact his punishment. Ten years, to be exact.

What if he had been wrong, though? No! He couldn't think that way. That would mean that the last ten years of anger, self-pity, and visions of revenge had been all for nothing. He couldn't accept that.

The elevator dinged and opened before he was able to say anything else, which was probably a good thing. He wasn't sure what would have come from his lips next.

Walking stiffly beside him, Jasmine didn't utter another

word as he led her to his vehicle, assisted her inside, and then drove them to an upscale café he frequented.

Knowing the staff well, he was able to obtain a private table in the back of the restaurant. He liked the place for its privacy when he needed to talk to a client or take a date out. Right now, he laughed to himself, he might need the privacy for when Jasmine launched herself across the table with a knife in her hand aimed at his cold heart.

The thought didn't terrify him at all. All he could see was her landing in his lap, her core positioned perfectly over his hardening body.

Yes, she could launch herself at him, knife or no knife. He could take her. And he would.

CHAPTER TEN

J ASMINE LOOKED GRIMLY around at the intimate restaurant. It was the middle of the afternoon, and there were candles burning on the tables. She threw another disgusted look at Derek's back as she followed him to the private table in the corner of the room.

If he really thought he could seduce her, he was going to be sorely disappointed.

The hostess sat them down and then asked what they would like to drink. He ordered an iced tea. Normally Jasmine didn't drink alcohol, especially in the middle of her workday, but she had the feeling she was going to need something much stronger than soda if she was going to make it through the rest of the day without either snapping at him or throwing her ice water in his face.

"I'll take a glass of red wine," she said with a smile. He raised his eyebrows but didn't say anything. She was testing his limits, seeing how far she could push him. Let's see if he'd fire her for having a glass of wine at the "business" lunch he'd forced her to endure with him.

Silence hung heavy over the two of them as they waited for their drinks, neither one willing to break the stalemate. When their appetizers arrived, Jasmine found that she was starving. Still without saying a word, she pulled some of the little nibbles onto her plate, then moaned just a bit. The food was excellent, and it disappeared quickly.

Derek's eyes widened slightly at her enthusiasm in attacking a meal that she hadn't wanted in the first place, but lucky for him, he didn't say a word. They ate in an uncomfortable silence for several more minutes before he cleared his throat. Apparently he'd have to be the one to say the first word.

"How long have you been doing HR?" he asked as he speared a piece of cold asparagus.

Jasmine could have continued to give him the cold shoulder, but the glass of wine she'd drunk had relaxed her, and as her initial hunger was abated, she decided she could play nice.

"I finished school four years ago and have been doing it ever since."

He seemed to calculate in his head before asking. "Did you take some time off before going to college?"

Jasmine barely managed to stop the answer she'd been about to give him. Yes, she'd taken time off — she'd had a newborn baby.

"I wanted a break after high school, so I waited a year before going back. Then I only went part time for the first year." She looked down at her plate and focused on her meal. As a general rule, Jasmine really hated lying. It just wasn't the time to tell him about Jacob yet. In any case, she wasn't really lying; she was just leaving out a few details.

"For some people that works out just fine," Derek said. "Others never get back to college. It was difficult for me to study, but I worked days and went to school at night. I knew I had to learn more if I wanted to change my life."

Jasmine looked up at the unguarded expression on his face. He was impassioned when speaking about those years. Some of her bitterness faded just a little. They'd been so young back then. If she'd forced him to listen to her that night they were supposed to run away together, would things have been different?

That was something she would never know.

During the rest of the meal the two of them stayed on the safe subject of school and managed to relax. When she excused herself to go to the restroom, she realized she wasn't having a horrible time — the opposite, in fact. As Jasmine was running a brush through her hair, her mouth dropped open when she looked in the mirror and her eyes connected with Amy's as the woman approached her from behind.

"I see you're getting *very* cozy with the boss," Amy said with an unreadable look in her eyes. Realizing now that she hadn't seen the woman in the office the last few days, Jasmine wondered what she was doing there at the restaurant.

"It's a business lunch, not that it's any of your business," Jasmine said, and then she made to go around her. She had no desire whatsoever to chat.

"It looked a lot cozier than a business lunch," Amy told her. "I wouldn't get too comfortable with Derek if I were you, though. He likes to add notches to his bedpost, but he gets bored quickly and then tosses you out even faster."

Jasmine just had to stare. Amy was one of his castoffs. Another one. Her horrified thoughts must have registered on her face because Amy's lips tilted up even more.

"I see the light is dawning. Yes, we've been intimate a long time. I'm actually expecting him to propose marriage at any moment, but it seems he wants to sow some more oats before settling down." Amy faced the mirror, pulling out a tube of bright red lipstick and carefully applying it as if she didn't have a care in the world.

"How could you want to be with a man who won't be faithful to you?" Jasmine asked. Maybe she was a little too naïve for the more hardened business world, but was she so foolish to worry about such a trait as fidelity?

"He can have his flings *now* — once he puts that ring on my finger, he will be mine and I'll make sure he doesn't go out to find whores," Amy said blithely. The look she sent Jasmine's way implied that Jasmine was one of those whores. The woman walked out of the bathroom, leaving Jasmine staring after her.

Jasmine looked at her own reflection in the mirror and shook her head. The woman was obviously trying to get a reaction from her, but why? It was true that Jasmine knew nothing about Derek, but she couldn't imagine that what Amy was saying was true.

Even if it weren't true, it was still a reminder to her that she couldn't let down her guard around Derek. Just because she'd had a pleasant meal with him didn't erase the past, didn't change the fact that he'd so coldly dismissed her ten years before.

It was time for her to pull herself together and remember that he was just her boss now. It was unfortunate, but that was their new relationship until she was able to find new work. Putting on a professional mask — the same one she'd used for years around her overbearing father — she walked from the bathroom and found Derek waiting at the table.

He seemed curious about her lengthy absence but was polite enough not to say anything. Gathering her purse, she didn't bother waiting for him to pay, but just turned and walked from the table to the front doors. She didn't need or want Derek to buy her lunch, feeling uncomfortable with him doing it now, even if it was a business lunch. She'd been taking care of herself for a long time, and she couldn't afford to lean on anyone else, not even for a meal.

Especially Derek Titan.

CHAPTER ELEVEN

DEREK TOOK CARE of the bill and met Jasmine out at the front curb. Something had happened between the time she'd left the table and the time she'd come back from the bathroom, and he couldn't figure out what it could be. She'd been starting to relax around him and then…

But, hey. It served his purposes better when she was on her guard. When she was being charming, it was too easy to forget who and what she was. It was too easy to forget what she'd done both to him and to his father.

They rode back to the office building in silence, and the elevator carrying only the two of them was filled with tension as the numbers slowly blinked for each passing floor. He heard her let out a sigh of relief when the doors opened, and she jumped out as if the hounds of hell were after her. He enjoyed the sway of her hips as he followed her along the hallway to his office.

The room was unusually warm, and he knew how Pavlov's dogs felt when she slipped her jacket off, revealing a silky tank-style blouse. It dipped in front to show the smallest hint of cleavage, increasing his desire to see more. The way her outfit hugged her body and showed her small waist off to perfection was exquisite torture. She'd grown curvier with age and now had a woman's body instead of the slim figure of a teenager.

His mouth went dry and his breathing escalated. He fought not to grab hold of her and feel how those curves would feel within his hands. Time had been good to her — her breasts would now spill from his palms. The perfect fit of his trousers was once again compromised, so he quickly sat down.

Jasmine picked up another file, getting right back to work. It was probably best for both of them.

"I need a break from looking at those folders. I'm going to start calling in people for some interviews," Derek told her. "Move over here to my desk and grab a notebook. I want you to jot down some notes. We'll start with your good friend Henry," he said with a grimace. He wanted to get a gander at the guy before throwing him out on his butt.

"That's fine with me. After all, *you're* the boss," she said with a bit too much sugar dripping from her tone.

His eyes grew cold. He really didn't like being mocked — perhaps a holdover from his youth. He was tempted to give her a lesson or two about what it meant to mess with him.

Instead, he called Henry and told him to report to the office immediately. Jasmine glared at him as he hung up.

"You really don't have to be so rude all of the time," she couldn't help saying.

Derek let it go because there was a knock at the door. The man was quick — maybe because he wasn't doing any work.

"Hello, Mr. Titan. I'm Henry Andrews." Henry came forward with his hand out. Derek shook it and then gave the man an assessing look. Henry was in his late thirties and what women would consider good-looking. His job was slipping through his fingers, and the poor guy had no clue.

"Jasmine! I was wondering where you've been," Henry said when he spotted her. He walked over and kissed her on the cheek. Derek was starting to see red again. He couldn't care less what the guy had to say. He was going to be fired. It took all of Derek's strength not to physically throw Henry out the door and tell him never to set foot on the premises again.

"As you know, Henry, we have to let a number of our employees go. There's always a lot of turnover when a company is taken over. You have a few minutes to tell me what it is you do here and defend your job," Derek said in a tone dripping with ice.

He could feel Jasmine's eyes burn holes through him. Yes, he was being even more cruel than usual, but he'd taken an instant dislike to this fellow, and the guy was toast anyway. Why bother to play nice?

"What Derek meant to say is we're reviewing all the files of the employees and know you're a valuable member of the team. Can you talk about your work?" she asked in a reassuring manner.

Derek wanted to shout at her. *That wasn't what I meant at all!* But he knew he'd sound like a child throwing a tantrum. He sat down in his chair and pointed his cold eyes directly at Henry, who was either clueless to his aggression or just pretending not to notice.

Henry started talking about his position in the marketing department. He listed his projects and the various tasks he currently had in the works. He laid out projects that he'd wanted to implement for months, but which had been ignored. Derek's mood sank further when he found that the man really knew what he was talking about and was actually a major asset.

Henry placed his portfolio on the desk, and Derek glanced through the organized notes. It was clear that David had been holding Henry back, and Derek figured that the only reason Henry had stuck around was to be near Jasmine; the man's talents were being wasted, to be sure. As much as he wanted to throw Henry out, he needed to have a cool head first.

He'd never once let a woman get between him and the bottom line, and Henry could definitely help his business. Keeping a poker face, Derek stood up to thank him for coming in. Then he sent him away. "We'll let you know our decision by tomorrow," he said, reverting to the corporate *we*.

As soon as Henry left the room, Jasmine turned on him. She walked stiffly toward him, and rage lit up her eyes. He was unbelievably aroused by the picture she made.

"How dare you act like a horse's ass, you pompous corporate drone?" she shouted.

She was less than a foot away as she stared him down. He'd seen her angry before, but her fury right now looked flammable. His own anger was rising to the surface as they stood. How dare she talk to him like that? He was the wronged one! He was also her boss.

He pressed the button down on his phone. "I want no interruptions in this room. I don't care if the place is on fire," he growled. And with the rage blowing through the room at that moment, fire was a distinct possibility.

"Yes sir," came the reply, and then the connection went dead.

He started moving toward Jasmine in a slow and measured stride. She seemed to realize her predicament, and she began to retreat fast. Her eyes grew wide, and he felt her temper evaporate. He must have looked frightening; he'd completely lost his cool.

She was the one who left him because he was poor. *She* was the one who thought she was still Miss High and Mighty. *She* was the one throwing her new boyfriend in his face. He couldn't even think, he was so furious.

He backed her up until her legs hit the table, and she stood pressed up against the hard surface. There was no escape. Her breath quickened, making her breasts rise and fall faster as they brushed against his chest. Her cheeks were flushed, and her lips were swollen from her nervous chewing.

Her eyes were still rounded in fear. If it had been only fear, he might have been able to squelch his anger, but he also saw excitement in their depths. She clearly still wanted him, but she was fighting herself as much as she was fighting him. He needed her.

Now!

He felt a low growl rumble in his throat and then he crushed his lips against hers. Grabbing her neck to pull her closer, he then pushed his tongue against her lips, demanding entrance.

She reached her hand up to push him away, but instead she ended up gripping his shirt. She couldn't stop her body's betrayal as she melted against him while his lips turned from almost abusive to seductive. He penetrated her mouth and then tangled his tongue with hers.

Liquid heat began pooling in her core as Derek deepened the kiss and pulled her so close to his hard chest that she could hardly tell where her body left off and his began. Her hands slipped up behind his neck, and she found herself pulling him even closer.

She heard him groan. Anger had quickly turned to blinding need, and she pressed her aching core against his arousal as she sought relief. Shock overtook her when she heard another groan and realized it was coming from her.

He suddenly grabbed her hips and sat her on the table, moving so he could fit between her thighs. Her silky skirt slid out of the way, and then he was pulling her forward. The table was the perfect height — he fit against her in the most intimate way possible. He ground his erection against her core, needing no barriers between their two bodies.

He couldn't think beyond anything but his need. He was hungry, and only she could satisfy him. He broke the kiss long enough to trail his lips down her neck. Then he whisked the blouse off her in seconds and gasped in pleasure at the scrap of lace that was barely covering her luscious breasts. They were spilling from the material, begging for his touch.

He didn't disappoint her. He unlatched her bra and then cupped the glorious weight in his hands as he brought his head down to take her hardened dusky-pink nipple into his mouth. He sucked the bud deep inside and twirled his tongue around the peak. His erection jumped as she groaned out her pleasure.

The noises of ecstasy were quickly pushing him to completion. He couldn't think. Hell, he could barely stand there!

He moved his head to ravish her other nipple and then brought his lips back up to hers, no longer able to keep from kissing her. As he continued to possess her mouth with years of pent-up passion, he undid his pants and then ripped her tiny panties away. The light went on in his head long enough for him to remember to fumble inside his wallet and quickly sheath himself, and then he was pressed against her hot folds. She moaned her approval.

He reached down to feel whether she was ready for him. She was wet, hot and tight, and he couldn't wait one second longer. He removed his hand and, with one quick thrust, drove deep inside her.

He groaned in ecstasy as her tight folds gripped him. He wasn't going to last long — not after fantasizing about this very moment for ten long years. He continued to kiss her as he grabbed her hips and thrust deeply in and out. She was crying out in pleasure as he pushed his long length inside her body, her stomach trembling against his own.

Fire ran through him as he reconnected with the first girl he'd felt any emotion toward. For she had been a girl before. She was all woman now. She cried out, and then he felt her tight heat start gripping him in convulsions. Her entire body began shaking, and that was all it took to send him over the edge. He groaned as he found his release while locked deep inside her.

As his body continued shuddering, he kept them joined until the very last spasm ran through each of them. When he was completely depleted, he reluctantly pulled back and then stared down at her. She was flushed, sitting there on the table, with her beautiful breasts exposed and her mouth swollen from his kisses.

Her normally perfect hair was pulled free of the bun, and, with her cheeks flushed, she was the most gorgeous creature he'd ever seen. She looked as if she'd just been devoured, which made him want to start all over again.

He was leaning down to kiss her, already feeling at a loss without her touch. Her expression changed from one of complete satisfaction to horror at what she'd done. He knew without a doubt that the moment was over, and now was the time for consequences.

She reached her hand up and slapped him hard across the face before he knew what was happening. The sting of it woke him up from the daze he'd been in. Bringing his hand up to his cheek to feel the heat, he could only look at her in shock. But then he couldn't help but smile at the strength she'd exhibited. He'd never had a woman give quite that reaction after sex. They were usually purring with utter contentment, if he did say so himself.

He quickly took a step back because smiling had been the wrong thing to do. He could see the fury building in her. "Sorry about that, Jasmine, but you can't blame the whole thing on me. You didn't say anything to stop me," he said, with just a bit too much smugness.

He was feeling anything but calm, but there was no way he'd show that. If he'd thought one time was going to be enough to wash her from his system, he'd been very wrong. It would take being with her for a while before he was able to finally let her go. Just the thought of entering her tight heat again was raising his blood pressure, among other things.

"How bloody dare you, you despicable excuse for a human being!" She turned his voice into that of a mincing wimp as she mocked his words. "'*Sorry about that, Jasmine. I just couldn't manage to keep my Johnson in my pocket. But since you didn't say no, it's perfectly all right.*' It's more than obvious that you haven't changed or grown up in ten years. Yes, I may have had a temporary meltdown, but that doesn't give you an excuse to do what you did. You're power hungry and think you own everything and everyone," she spit out.

Jasmine gathered up her clothing, looking down at her torn panties with dismay, and then walked into his private bathroom and shut the door with a resounding click. She didn't slam it in a fit of rage, as so many women might have done; the click made much more of a statement. She didn't reappear for some time.

Derek was grateful for the time to collect his wits, especially after her scathing words. He felt a little lower than pond scum right then.

When she finally came out of the bathroom, her face was a mask. No one would have been able to tell she'd just come apart in his arms. Derek smiled ruefully as he realized that she was almost as good as he was at wearing a mask.

"That will not happen again," she said in a cold, professional tone. She'd have been furious to know that he looked at her words as a challenge, and, of course, he'd never been able to resist a challenge.

He said nothing — once bitten, after all. He was surprised she didn't go stomping out of the office, trying to yell sexual harassment. And she might well have had a good case against him, but even if she hadn't, just the headlines would be deadly. Instead, she sat down at the table and started going through the files again as if nothing had happened.

That took his pride down just a notch.

When he realized he'd been standing there uselessly for several moments, he moved to his desk, called the secretary and had some beverages brought in, and then he had her leave the door open. He didn't trust himself to be all alone with Jasmine, locked up in the office, for the rest of the afternoon. He was having a hell of a time knowing she was right there next to him with absolutely nothing on underneath that skirt. But what did that say about him as a man?

She had him on the ropes...just as she had ten years earlier.

Derek pushed all such thoughts from his mind, and they spent the rest of the day calling people into the office for interviews. He wasn't pleased to find her correct about most of the people who came in. Those she'd fought to save were smart and knew how to do their jobs. The only one he was really struggling with letting go was Henry.

At five on the dot Henry poked his head in the door. "Hey, I don't want to interrupt, but I forgot to tell you that Gina wanted to invite you over this weekend for some candle party thing she's throwing," he said to Jasmine.

She laughed her first real laugh since Derek had stepped back into her life. "Tell her I would love to come. Can I bring anything?" she asked.

"She also told me to tell you not to bring a thing. She made sure I enforce that, since you always go out of your way to make your own parties amazing. She said it's her turn to pamper you a bit," he added with a smile.

"OK, I get it. Tell her I can't wait, and I'll see you both this weekend."

"No way am I staying with all you ladies. No offense, but I'm taking off for the day with the guys to do some shooting." Henry then turned and left the room. Derek felt more than a little bit stupid now — the guy was obviously married.

At least he wouldn't have to fire him. He thought he might even finagle an invitation to go shooting with Henry and his friends, just so he could swing by the house and check up on Jasmine. She stood up and gathered her jacket.

"We aren't done yet," he said.

"I'm done. I have something to do tonight. It's my normal quitting time, and all the other employees are leaving. There's nothing that will not hold until tomorrow. Fire me if you want. I don't care anymore." She didn't wait for his response but just marched out of the room.

He sat there, a little stunned and a little turned on, and he wasn't sure which emotion was stronger. He decided to call it a day, too, and collected what he needed before heading out.

His mind was on Jasmine the entire elevator ride down, and the entire ride home. He was supposed to be finding sweet revenge, and instead, she was once again the one in charge of their relationship.

It was just a damn good thing that she didn't know that.

CHAPTER TWELVE

W HEN DEREK GOT home, he was delighted to see his cousin Drew sitting in the den with a drink in his hand and a smile on his face. They were closer than any brothers could possibly be.

"I'm going to have to talk to the footman again about keeping the riffraff out of here," Derek said.

"Yeah, I know what you mean. It seems like they will let any old bum in off the street nowadays. Home security here is nonexistent," Drew replied.

"At least we agree," Derek said.

"How are you doing, cuz?" Drew asked.

"I'm great, Drew, and you?"

"Well, since I found your sixty-four-year-old scotch, I'm feeling pretty good." With an impish smile, Drew held up the expensive bottle, which had considerably less liquid in it than it had boasted in the morning, when Derek had left for work.

"OK. If you're going to drink my best stuff, then the least you can do is pour me a glass," Derek said as he shed his jacket and tie and rolled up his sleeves.

"No problem. How's the corporate-takeover world treating you?" Drew asked as he handed him the glass.

"I finally got my company," Derek said with a genuine smile. He didn't have to explain what that company was. Drew had grown up with him. He'd been there when Jasmine left him, when her father had destroyed his dad's chances of a real business, and he'd been there by his side as Derek had plotted his revenge.

Drew was from the same impoverished neighborhood as Derek, and he had been just as determined to get out. It had always been the two of them and their other cousin, Ryan. Their fathers were all brothers, so they shared the same last name. Ryan's parents had died in a terrible auto accident when he was ten years old, and he'd moved in with Drew, next door to Derek. The three boys had been inseparable.

They'd all left when they were twenty years old and made successes of their lives. They stayed in touch, at least as much as their work would allow. Sometimes Derek hated the distance that divided them now that they were older.

"That's beyond great, Derek. How did it all happen?" Drew asked with genuine interest.

"David was a very poor businessman, and all I had to do was bide my time and wait him out. He finally made one too many mistakes, leaving the doors wide open for me to come in and take over. It feels great, but I thought I would somehow feel more — like some completion or closure or something."

"Too much psychobabble to share with your wonderful scotch. But here's the thing. I think you're just growing up, and getting revenge isn't as important as it once used to be for you. What are you going to do with this one?"

"I've decided to keep it intact. The product is actually top quality, and there are over five hundred factory employees who would lose their jobs if I divided it up. I think they will do a spectacular job once they are getting paid what they really should be," Derek answered.

"Turning softhearted on me, huh? What happened to my coldhearted snake of a cousin?"

"I guess, like you said, I've grown up and can think beyond myself once in a while," Derek said, a bit uncomfortable with what counted for praise with his cousins.

"Don't worry. I won't tell your secrets to the world. They can all think you're still a jackal," he said and then punched Derek in the arm.

"OK. Enough about me, Drew. It's been too long since we last talked. Tell me what you've been up to," Derek demanded.

"I just got back from Spain. We opened up another resort. You'll have got to come stay there, because she's a beauty." Drew pulled out a folder, and Derek looked through the pictures. It was certainly an impressive place, with all the bells and whistles. "It has three Olympic-size pools, a full-use spa, a couple of top-of-the-line workout rooms and so much more. It's a woman's paradise and a man's dream. Or vice versa. I should get an award for this place," Drew said.

Derek decided he'd take a vacation there once he finished dealing with the current employee situation. He'd seen the beginning phases of this new resort and hadn't realized it had been so long since he'd spoken to his cousin.

Derek was used to staying in some nice spots, but for the last five years he'd stayed at his cousin's places whenever he could. He liked to review the service for Drew, since Drew wasn't able to be in every place at once, but he also genuinely liked the resorts. They were world class, and he got better service than he would at any regular hotel.

At first, he'd been able to stay at them without the staff knowing who he was, and he could give an honest assessment to his cousin, but his name was just too big now, and the employees knew him the moment he walked through the doors. It didn't matter. The service was always exceptional, whether they knew who he was or not.

"She's my favorite so far. You know, it's a hard life traveling to all these exotic places." Drew sighed, but he couldn't contain the huge grin that split his face apart. The boys had never been out of the state of Washington until they hit their twenties…

"I seriously need to allow myself more vacations. Now that I've acquired Freeman Industries and turned it into Titan Medical, I can slow down a bit," Derek said. He was only thirty years old, but he had experienced so much in his life, he felt far older.

"Yeah, I think I see a few gray hairs in there," Drew goaded him.

"I may be a few months older than you, but I can still kick your ass," Derek said with a wink.

"Yeah, I'm really scared. OK, let's get out of here. I need a greasy burger and a beer. This scotch is all right, but sometimes a cold bottle of dark brew is the only thing that hits the spot," he said before he emptied his glass.

"Sounds great to me, Drew. Work has been stressful, and it will be nice to unwind at a grease joint, away from sharks in white collars."

"Like you?" Drew asked.

Derek guffawed and ran quickly up the stairs to change into his favorite pair of worn jeans and a T-shirt. He slapped on his favorite baseball cap, then smiled as he looked in the mirror. The people he dealt with in the corporate world wouldn't recognize him in his off-time clothing. He liked it that way. It reminded him of his roots.

Luckily, he never ran into any of the big suits in his favorite dive, which happened to be a country music bar that played some of the best undiscovered talent around. He'd even helped a few of the bands, without their knowledge, by sending in their music to some of his connections.

The boys jumped into Drew's big Ford pickup truck and headed out. The bar was about an hour's drive when there wasn't a lot of traffic. During rush hour it could take several hours. Luckily, the traffic wasn't bad, and they were sitting at a table in no time at all.

They each ordered burgers, fries and beer, and then sat back to listen to the band play. This was one of the few places Derek knew of that played live music seven days a week, and it was always good.

The surroundings worked their needed magic on his mood. He managed to push his stress away and enjoy the conversation with his cousin. From its rocky beginnings, the day was turning out to be one of the best he'd had in too long to remember.

He was sitting back, digesting his food and sipping on his beer, when his cousin interrupted his semi-comatose state.

"Have you seen Jasmine yet?" Drew asked. Derek started choking on the sip of beer he'd just taken and Drew pounded his back while he struggled to get his breath back. "I guess that's a yes."

"She works for the corporation," Derek finally managed to get out.

"Whoa, how's that working out? Have you fired her yet?" Drew asked. He was well acquainted with the reasons behind Derek's long-planned revenge.

"No, I haven't fired her. I want her to regret dumping me, regret helping her dad hurt mine, before I toss her out on her butt," he said. The thought of tossing her out was less and less appealing the more time he spent with her, but he didn't want to think about that now.

His cousin raised his eyebrows and studied Derek. "I see," Drew said, a pasted smile on his face.

"What do you see?" Derek demanded to know.

"You're falling for the girl again, instead of the other way around," Drew goaded.

"You don't know what you're talking about," Derek snapped. He was angry, more with himself than with Drew, because he thought there might be some truth to his cousin's words.

"Hey, it's been ten years, and people can change," Drew said.

"I won't forget what she did to me, and worse, what she did to Dad," Derek said to both Drew and himself.

"Even at the time, you didn't really think that what

happened to your dad's loan was really her idea. She probably just thought things were going too fast, and her father took it too far. Just because she wanted to back out of the relationship, that didn't mean she wanted to destroy you."

"Whatever," Derek growled. Drew and Ryan had always loved Jasmine, and it was one of the reasons Derek had loved her so much. She'd just been so good to his family — until that last day.

"Anyway, you're a smart guy, Derek. Go with your gut, and you'll know what to do," Drew told him. Even though the world saw Derek as a playboy who couldn't take anything seriously, he was actually highly intelligent and the most caring man Derek and Ryan knew. They were allowed to see a side of Drew no one else got to see. "Besides, cuz, I always thought Jasmine was a real catch."

"Yeah, a real catch who despised me and my empty pockets."

"I still think the two of you were meant to be together. Maybe fate is finally stepping in. Maybe she's all grown up."

"OK. Enough of this emotional crap. Let's get out of here, head back to my place, and drink too much," Derek said.

Drew took the hint and backed off. They paid the bill, leaving the waitress a generous tip, and then headed out to the truck for the drive back.

Derek's mood quickly mellowed as they made the commute home. He knew his cousin meant well and wasn't trying to get a reaction, but it made him think too much about what his intentions really were toward Jasmine. She was the one who got away, and he hoped he was strong enough this time around to not let her break him.

He knew he was certainly more mature, but he seemed to revert right back to his childhood when he looked into those dark brown eyes of hers. She had a way of knocking his feet right out from under him. He'd harden himself back up by the time he returned to the office. And he didn't mean *harden* the way it had turned out less than eight hours before.

Hell, for that matter, he was needed there for only a few more days before his competent staff could assume full oversight of the operation. He could monitor the company from his main office and not have to see Jasmine much. Damn, why didn't that sound more appealing? He was going to have to put some distance between them, and fast.

He decided he'd do that once he got her out of his system for the last time. He needed to take her to bed a couple of times more, and then he'd lose interest. He always lost interest once the chase was over.

That was it. All figured out. He wasn't still in love with her. He was just enjoying the chase.

Even if he had an inkling that he was full of crap, he managed to make himself feel better by the time they reached his place. With a smile of anticipation for the week to come, he walked in his door. Game on.

CHAPTER THIRTEEN

J ASMINE ARRIVED AT the school just in time to pick Jacob up. He came running down the hallway and gave her a big hug, since no one else happened to be around. She loved the rare moments when he let himself go and allowed her to hold him.

They were getting fewer and far between the older he got.

"How was your practice?" she asked.

"It was really cool. I pinned Timmy in, like, three seconds."

"Good job, Little Man. Did you get up and give him a handshake afterward?"

"Of course, Mom," he said with exasperation and a slight eye roll. She'd taught her son well, and she loved that being polite was second nature to him. She hated to see men, or women for that matter, gloat over their victories.

Now if she could just get his eye-rolling under control, he'd be a perfect child.

"Timmy asked if I could stay the night on Friday. He has a birthday party, and they're going to Skate World," he told her, his excitement overflowing.

"I'll talk to Timmy's mom and make sure it's OK, but I don't see any reason why you can't stay with him."

"Thanks, Mom. You're the best," he said with a smile that transformed his face into looking so much like his father, it actually pierced her gut. The older Jacob got, the more he looked like Derek. She prayed they never met, because the resemblance was far too great to be passed aside as coincidence.

It didn't help that Jacob now liked his hair in a style that was almost the image of Derek's haircut. But she shook off those thoughts and ruffled his thick mane, then walked by his side as they left the building.

Jacob's coach approached them outside. "How are you doing, Jasmine?"

"I'm doing well. And how are you, Chuck?"

"Just great. Jacob forgot to grab one of these fliers. We have a tournament on Saturday, starting at four," he said.

"That sounds like fun. Is there anything I can bring?"

"I always know I can count on you," he said with a laugh. "Would it be too much to ask for you to bring a main course for an after-meet meal? I have some people bringing drinks and fruit, but no one signed up for a main course. You can do sandwiches if you want, but I know you like to get all fancy," he said with a flirty smile.

She was well known for her crowd-pleasing dishes, and that's most likely why no one else had signed up for the spot.

"You know me well," she said with a laugh. "Of course I'll whip up something. I have to make sure these boys get plenty of nourishment. Those long tournaments take a lot out of nine-year-olds."

She could see that Chuck was trying to work up the courage to ask her out again, but after her afternoon with Derek, she had no desire for such a date. She felt trapped, and she tried to think of something to say, anything, to avoid his question. She wasn't sure whether she wanted to close this door with Chuck. It had been ten years since she'd been close with a man, and it was time for her to move forward with her life, but with Derek around her now, her thoughts were all muddled.

"Have you seen that new action flick with Bruce Willis?" he asked as if it were just polite conversation.

"Isn't he getting too old to be in action films?"

"Are you kidding me? The guy is in the best shape of his life," Chuck said with a laugh. "If you don't count the hair."

"I have to admit, he's still a big crush of mine," she admitted. "And hair is sometimes overrated."

"I'm shocked, Miss Freeman," he said.

"I know. I know. But, I've been a bit in love ever since the first "Die Hard" movie. It's getting late, though, Chuck, so I'd better get Jacob home so he can get his homework started. I hope you have a great night." She turned quickly away so he wouldn't have an excuse to extend the conversation.

As Jasmine and Jacob made their way to her car, she heard Chuck call out a goodbye, but she just lifted her hand in the air and waved, not turning around. She had to make some decision about him, but just not now.

"It sounds like you're going to have a very busy weekend," she said to her son as they drove toward home.

"I know. I can't wait for the party. Trevor said he was having an ice-cream cake," Jacob said, practically bouncing in his seat.

"Just remember that you're wrestling the next day, so if you eat too much junk food, you'll get sick at your meet and throw up all over your opponents."

"That would be so cool!" he exclaimed.

Jasmine shook her head — sometimes boys just made no sense at all. Speaking to them was like talking in another language entirely.

"OK, Jacob. Remember I warned you when you're feeling sick come Saturday afternoon," she said with her mom's knowing grin. The boy rolled his eyes — *not again!* she thought — but remained silent.

When they arrived home, she made them both a good dinner and then tossed a ball with him in the backyard. She loved it when Seattle's weather saw fit to cooperate and she could spend time outdoors with her son.

She needed to save up some money and take Jacob on a vacation in the winter to get away from the gloomy skies. The lack of sunlight wasn't good for anyone's mood, and that wasn't fair to Jacob or her.

They played catch until they couldn't see anymore; she prayed it was enough exertion to allow her a restful night of sleep. She was dreading going into the office the next day, but she'd do it with her head held high if she had her wits about her.

But the exercise wasn't enough. That night, as she lay in bed, her body refused to shut down. Each time she closed her eyes, all she could think about was Derek's talented fingers caressing her body, his hard shaft filling her so perfectly.

She should be outraged, horrified at her behavior, but instead she was hot and needy and just wanted more. What would it take for her to get over the man who had shattered her heart? Wasn't one crushing rejection enough to make her stay away from him?

Apparently not, because after just a few days in his presence, she was allowing him inside her heart again — and fool her twice, shame on her.

CHAPTER FOURTEEN

J ASMINE WALKED THROUGH those wretched doors once again and slowly made her way toward the elevator. She considered taking the stairs, just to delay the inevitable, but she didn't think she'd be able to breathe by the time she hit the twenty-fifth floor.

At least it was Friday. She could make it through one more day. The last two had been filled with unbelievable sexual tension — for her, at least. She didn't think Derek had thought about their time on his table since he'd pulled up his pants. He'd barely even looked at her. But that was a good thing, wasn't it?

She lectured herself all the way to the top of the building. She could get through one more day. They were down to their last few files. Then he'd most likely return to the head office, and she could relax. Work would go back to normal, and her life would resume just as it had been before his sudden reappearance.

She jumped when the bell on the elevator rang. The doors opened, and she walked out feeling as if she were on the green mile, taking her final steps toward the execution room. She didn't even bother going into her office. She knew that the second she sat down, Derek would buzz her and demand she get to his office pronto.

The strap of her bag slipped down her shoulder, but with her hands burdened by takeout coffee, she could do nothing about it. She stepped into Derek's office and sighed. Of course he was there ahead of her. The man never slept late or showed up even two minutes past seven in the morning.

She'd been used to being the first one at work in the morning, but it was impossible with him around, and she couldn't arrive any earlier, since she had to get her son off to school. She set the extra coffee cup down in front of him and then took her place at the table, looking at the much smaller pile of personnel folders.

"Thanks," Derek muttered, and he grabbed the cup without so much as looking up. She had brought him one only because the day before, when she'd come in with a large caramel macchiato, he'd thrown down a fifty and told her to bring him one, too, the next morning, since she was stopping anyway.

He hadn't bothered to ask her whether it would be inconvenient — hadn't bothered to ask, period. He'd just assumed she'd do it for him. It hadn't been a battle worth fighting, so she just picked up the coffee for him. It wasn't as if she had to go out of her way. Besides, he was now paying for hers too, and the morning boosts weren't cheap.

She'd live off the coffees and nothing else if she could get away with it. She had done that a day or two in the past, and, by the end, she was shaking all over, but, hey, her house had gotten incredibly clean.

"We have a couple of interviews more for today, with the last of the previous employees," Derek said. "I want you to go through the applications that have come in over the week and weed through them. Find the best candidates and schedule them for next week. We need to get those positions filled as soon as possible." He finally looked up.

Unfortunately for her, when he looked up, she was busy staring at inappropriate parts of his body. His eyebrows rose, and she couldn't suppress the deep flush that stained her cheeks. She turned away from him, praying he'd just pretend it hadn't happened.

She needed to get out of his office because every time she looked at the table, she pictured herself sitting there with him between her thighs. She nodded her head and then pretended to be engrossed with the file in front of her.

DEREK COULD FEEL himself tightening the second Jasmine walked into the room. No matter how subtle her scent was, he was sure he could pick it out even in a room filled with overperfumed socialites. He'd grown to crave her fragrance, and he wanted to bury his head in her shoulder, just draw the smell of her in. Hell, he wanted to bury himself in certain other areas of her body as well.

When he looked up to see her eyes on the very body part he wanted to sink into her, it took all of his many years of brutal self-control not to grab her and have a repeat performance of the one earlier in the week. He found himself actually gripping the desk to keep from bounding over to her and pouncing like a randy teenager.

Instead, he managed to keep it professional. They called in the last four employees and kept only one of them on. The final interview wasn't going well.

"I appreciate your years of service with the former Freeman Industries, Andy, but Titan Medical has a different vision of the future, and I don't think we'll make a good fit together," Derek said.

"You sorry bastard! You come in here with your corporate takeover and replace most of the people without even blinking. You'll get what is coming to you!" the man shouted.

Andy was so angry, there was spit flying from the corner of his mouth. He stood up as if to come over and deck Derek, but Derek wasn't intimidated in the least. He stood up to his full height and narrowed his gaze at the man threatening him.

"I see you're nice and cozy with the enemy, Jasmine," Andy bellowed. "Your father would be so disappointed in you, but that's nothing new. He's always been disappointed. He only allowed you to keep the job here because he was too embarrassed to have you out in the workforce, sullying his good name. You have never done anything right. He's complained many times about you and your bastard son."

The second Andy turned on Jasmine, Derek lost his cool. He was going to punch out the man's lights and damn the consequences. He was walking over to do just that when the guy delivered his last line. Derek's head whipped toward Jasmine.

She had a son? How had he not known that? There was nothing in her files, but he'd thought he'd done more research on her. Apparently not. How old was this child? Was she still involved with the father? He felt as if he'd been kicked in the gut.

His temper exploded again when he saw her face. She was as white as a ghost and looked as if she was going to pass out.

"My father wouldn't have said that," she whispered.

"He's said that and so much more. He can barely tolerate you. You're so unbelievably naïve," the man spat and took a step toward her.

Derek broke out of his trance and grabbed Andy by his shirt. He lifted him off his feet and then tossed him toward the door, where the guy tripped and fell to the ground. "Get out of my building, and do it *now*. If you set foot in here again, or anywhere near Jasmine, charges will be filed." Rage had transformed Derek's features into a frightening mask; even his current adversary was smart enough not to push him any further.

Jasmine looked from him to the ex-employee and then back again. Derek saw the shock and fear written all over her face.

"Security," Derek yelled, which made her jump. Within two seconds, two men came in, took one look at Andy and hauled him to his feet, yanking him out of the office.

Once he was a distance away from Derek, Andy seemed to gain back an ounce of his courage. "This isn't over," he was screaming as they dragged him away.

Derek walked over to Jasmine and pulled her into his arms.

She resisted for a moment and then buried her head in his shoulder as the sobs started racking her body. She threw her arms around him and wept for a short moment. Women and tears generally roused only his disgust, but there was so much pain radiating from her that he couldn't do anything but try to offer comfort.

The jerk had relayed some really hateful things, and Derek was sure her father had said them all. She now was getting a taste of what a loathsome man he truly was. Derek had to guard himself, though, and not let his feelings get too soft for a woman he knew too well. She might appear different from ten years ago, but she had once tossed him out without a look back, and did people ever really change that much?

Jasmine, finally getting herself under control, seemed to realize that she was wrapped in his arms. Looking up at him with red-rimmed eyes and tearstained cheeks, she took a breath, gathering courage to speak. He was about to bring his hand up and wipe the tears away, when she drew back.

"I'm sorry," she hiccupped. She then pulled away, headed into the bathroom, and didn't emerge for a while. It gave him time to go to his computer. He had to do some research on her to find out what he could about her life. He wanted to know whether she'd been married when her son was born and if she was married now. He needed to know what was going on. But, really, she couldn't be married now, could she? She never would have allowed the sex to go forward if she was. Jasmine had been a virgin their first time — surely she couldn't have changed that much in ten years. Still, she'd fooled him once. He knew it was going to take a while, but he'd find the information he wanted.

Jasmine finally walked from the bathroom, looking much more composed.

"Derek, we've finished with all the interviews today, and I can easily take my laptop home and go through the applications. I haven't had a personal day in a long time and would really like to take one now. I wouldn't normally ask, but I would appreciate it if you would let me head out early today." Her shoulders were back and her head high. She was expecting an argument.

"That will be fine. Just have those names ready for me by Monday morning," he said, barely taking the time to look at her.

Jasmine grabbed her belongings and rushed out the door. She swung by her office and put together what she'd need over the weekend, and then she was out to her car within fifteen minutes.

By the time she walked in the door of her home and calmly set her belongings down, she knew it was time to place a call. Dialing her father's number from memory, she waited for the voice mail to beep. "Dad, this is Jasmine, and this will be my last call to you. Andy Lakenson got fired today and he told me some things you said about me. If you did say them, then you'll know what I'm talking about, and don't even bother to call me back, because I won't want to speak to you again. If you didn't say these vicious things, then you need to call me and explain why Andy would say you did. If I don't hear from you tonight, I guess that's my answer." There was no emotion in her voice as she spoke to his recorder. She was almost numb.

A man she'd always thought was a hero was turning out to be the monster others had told her he was, and the reality of her recent discoveries wasn't pleasant. Everything surrounding the takeover was crushing her.

When the phone rang a couple of hours later, she was reluctant to pick it up. But she squared her shoulders and lifted the handle, quietly saying hello.

"It's your father," he said curtly.

"Dad, what's going on? You haven't called me. You just disappeared, and now I'm hearing all this information that can't possibly be true." Jasmine was trying to keep her tone normal. Her father hated displays of emotion.

"I heard you've gotten cozy with the new boss," he spat at her, ignoring her questions.

"I'm trying to make the best of a bad situation," she said, shocked by his coldness.

"Well, you were always good at adapting, weren't you?" he said. He continued before she was able to say anything. "You don't leave me a message telling me not to call you. Not ever. If I want to call, I damn well will. I've put up with you for years, but I'm done now. It's because of you that I've lost everything. Your bastard of a boyfriend felt he had to take everything away, and now you're all cozy with him once more. I see where your loyalties lie."

"I'm not all cozy with him, Dad. I just need the job. I have a son to support," she told him.

"You're always full of excuses. You're no different now than you were as a child. I'm done coddling you. If you can get that man to back the hell off me, then you can call me. Otherwise, you can stay out of my life!" he shouted.

The phone went dead. Jasmine stared at the beeping receiver. What had just happened?

She had no more tears left, and that was a good thing — she had to pull herself together for her son's sake. She went to the bathroom to wash her face; when she looked in the mirror, she vowed she'd never get taken advantage of or be abused again.

CHAPTER FIFTEEN

DEREK HAD ALL calls held and sat at his desk, deep in his research. He soon learned that Jasmine had never been married. She didn't even appear to have been in a serious relationship. It took him a while to find information on her son, though, because he was working on the assumption he was a toddler.

When he realized how old the boy was, his heart seemed to stall. He was doing some important math in his head. No matter which way he looked at it, the date of the child's birth coincided with the time he'd been with her. He knew she'd been a virgin when they slept together, and he couldn't imagine she'd jumped from his bed into another man's within a couple of weeks' time.

He had no idea how many hours he sat there, trying to figure everything out. If he was a father, why hadn't she told him? Why hadn't she come after him for child support? He was a very wealthy man, and she could have tried to exploit that.

He'd been working with her for a week, and she hadn't said a word about her son. The only explanation seemed to be that he wasn't the father. But he didn't understand why she wouldn't try to pass the kid off as his. She knew the timing would work, and she might have thought he wouldn't demand a DNA test.

He needed to get some answers, and there was no way in hell he was waiting until Monday morning. Dammit, he was going to her house right now — where did she live, anyway? He looked up her address and was taken aback by the neighborhood. It wasn't the poorest area, but it certainly wasn't what she was used to. Hell, her father still lived in a mansion — well, he had until he was forced to place it on the market.

She lived in a modest neighborhood, and the house had about as much square footage as his bedroom. He didn't get it. None of this made any sense. All of his perceptions of her were being destroyed one by one. What he needed was hard answers.

Preparing to rush off, he glanced at the clock and learned to his utter frustration that it was close to midnight. He'd been sitting at his computer all day and night without any concept of time, and now he had no choice but to wait until the morning before talking to her. It was going to be a long, sleepless night.

Still, when he walked out to his car, he couldn't keep himself from driving in the direction of her place. He had to see if it was really in the type of neighborhood his search suggested. It took him about thirty minutes to reach the area, and it was exactly as he'd pictured.

He slowed his car and looked at the house numbers until

he spotted her place. It was a nice house for what it was. No one could say she lived in the slums, like the area he'd grown up in, but he was so used to luxury condos and high-rises that he'd almost forgotten what working-class neighborhoods looked like.

The place was a pale blue color with white trim. He glanced at the well-maintained lawn — which was due to be mowed soon — and the many flowers planted around it. The yard was surrounded by a white picket fence. *She lives in suburbia*, he thought, with an almost hysterical laugh.

Each house in the neighborhood was identical to hers, just different paint and the garage placed on opposite sides. Even when he was younger, he'd despised tract housing, but it was all the rage with people these days. Maybe he just had hated it back then because they couldn't afford it, and hated it now because it's where she'd chosen to live.

He'd dreamed of living in a place like that when he'd been growing up. He and his cousins would go walking through the neighborhoods, picking out which house they would own and exactly what cars would be parked in the driveway. His dreams had strayed a long way since those days. He now lived on the top floor of a huge complex, with no yard in sight and vehicles aplenty tucked away that bore no relation to the ones he'd lusted after in his youth.

Derek sat there in his car, wistfully thinking it would be nice to have a yard. Her place was far too small for his tastes, but he kept coming back to the idea of a yard. If the boy really did turn out to be his, he'd start looking for property to build a nice house on. Hell, even if the boy didn't turn out to be his, he was going to start looking. It was time to have some land and maybe a few horses and other animals roaming around.

He kept fighting with himself, because everything in him wanted to pound on her door and demand answers right now. He wasn't a patient man in the best of circumstances, and he needed to know whether he had a son. If it was true, he'd already lost over nine years of the boy's life, and he wasn't willing to lose one minute more.

He debated with himself for a few minutes and then decided there was no use causing a scene in the middle of the night. When he moved to start the car, there was a knock at his window. He normally wasn't a jumpy person, but his heart leapt as he turned to see the bright end of a flashlight.

He rolled his window down to see who was interrupting him in the middle of the night. He almost hoped it was a robber so he could have an excuse to take his frustrations out on someone.

"What are you doing parked out here, son?" a stern voice asked.

Derek had to suppress the smile that wanted to rise to his lips. Only in this type of area would an officer approach and call him *son*. If he'd been in the slums, the cop would be holding out a gun, and if he were in his high-rise area, the man would be showing him a lot more respect, considering the amount of money he put into the tax fund.

"Sorry, officer. I got lost and was looking at my iPad to figure out how to get turned around." The lie rolled easily off his lips.

"Let me see your license and registration. You can shut

the motor off while I check everything out," the officer said, suspicion dripping from every word. Derek had to admit he did look suspicious sitting in front of the home in the family neighborhood, especially in his Mercedes. The cop probably thought it was stolen, since he wasn't able to clearly see the custom suit Derek was still wearing.

And to give the guy credit, the cop wasn't too far off thinking he was a stalker, considering he was stalking Jasmine at this very moment.

"Here you go," Derek said, as he passed his information through the window. The officer looked at him again and then sidled back to his car. Derek was grateful the lights weren't flashing. He was praying Jasmine was asleep in her house and would never know of this.

Though he was still angry with her, he didn't need a confrontation in the middle of the night, with an officer as a witness and all the neighbors' porch lights flashing on.

The officer was gone about ten minutes, enough time to make Derek squirm a bit, as if he were back in high school and had just stolen the mayor's car. Yes, that was something he'd done, but it had been a prank. Of course, he'd been the one to get caught for it, and he'd had to sit in the small jail overnight while Drew and Ryan had been home watching horror flicks and eating chocolate.

He wasn't that stupid kid anymore and needed to pull himself together. He was now a respected member of the community, highly valued and pretty much revered wherever he went. It was all this dredging up of the past that was throwing him off. Once again, Jasmine was getting the better of him.

It was damn well going to stop — and stop right now.

"Mr. Titan, I apologize for all of this. Had you just let me know who you were…" The officer spoke as he came back to the window, looking slightly flustered. "Can I give you any directions?"

This was the way Derek was normally treated, what he was used to. It hadn't taken the officer long to figure out who he was.

"No, sir. I have it all figured out now," Derek said, just wanting to get on his way. This day had gone from bad to worse very quickly.

"Well, you have a great night." The officer turned and went back to his vehicle, then pulled back onto the road and disappeared.

Derek sighed before starting his car and driving off, soon hitting the main roads. He was wide awake and not thrilled to walk back into his empty place.

When he'd finally made it home, he reached into the back of a drawer in his desk and pulled out the photo he kept there, holding it beneath the light to gaze at the image.

It was of him and Jasmine, the summer he'd fallen in love with her. Many times he'd tried to toss out the old picture, but he'd never quite managed to talk himself into doing so. The sparkle in her eyes practically leapt from the still shot as her arm wrapped around his waist.

Drew had taken the picture, and his cousin had teased him mercilessly about his goofy grin.

Derek had been so in love with her, willing to walk to the

ends of the earth and back if she so commanded it of him.

Forcing himself to put away the worn photo, he stood and made his way to his bedroom. The night couldn't end soon enough for him, and the sooner he got to sleep, the sooner he'd get the answers he wanted.

CHAPTER SIXTEEN

J ASMINE WOKE UP to the sound of pounding. She wasn't a morning person at the best of times, and the insistent knocking on her door was making this one of the worst.

She climbed out of bed and stumbled down the stairs, not bothering to put on a robe to cover up her old T-shirt and tiny boxer shorts. If the jerk at the door was rude enough to wake her up early on a Saturday, whoever it was could deal with her bedtime apparel.

She knew her hair would be frightening and her eyes still only half slits. Perhaps she'd scare the unwanted visitor enough that he or she would never call so early again. She yanked open the door. "What do you want at this ungodly hour?" she snapped before looking up.

She gasped at the sight of Derek standing on her front porch. He didn't look happy. Well, that made two of them.

"Is that how you greet all your guests?" he asked with a mocking smile.

"Number one, you're not my guest," she fired back. "And number two, most people are too smart to show up at my doorstep at the break of dawn on a weekend." What could he possibly be doing there at all?

But her fuzzy brain was sidetracked. She detected the scent of coffee, and her eyes widened as she inhaled the wonderful aroma. He was holding two large cups, and she was fighting with herself — should she shut the door in his face, or make a grab for the cup first? She was awake now, and she wanted that coffee badly.

A smile threatened to spread across Derek's features when he saw the look of pure lust when Jasmine saw the java. He had to fight to suppress it. He'd made a last-minute decision to swing by and grab it because even after one week of working with her, he knew she wasn't a happy person until she'd downed at least a few cups. He'd learned to wait to speak to her until it was obvious that the caffeine had kicked in and was doing its magical job.

He held out the brew as a peace offering, forgetting for a moment that he was there to demand answers from her. She grabbed it and took a large gulp, sighing in pleasure as the coffee traveled down her throat.

He felt the sigh all the way down to his toes. Damn, she could go from almost frightening to downright erotic in a split second. He wanted that look to be on her face as he slipped deep inside her body. She'd certainly woken up one part of *his* anatomy.

"Um, thanks for the coffee. Now go away and come back at a decent hour," she said and began shutting the door in his face. He was so shocked at being dismissed in this way that he almost allowed her to slam the door. At the last second, he put his foot out.

"I need to talk to you," he almost growled.

"Whatever it is, it can wait until Monday morning. I brought my work home and will have everything ready for you then," she said. "Sheesh, Derek."

So she thought he was there about work. Well, he reasoned with himself, what else would she think he was there for?

"I'm coming in, Jasmine. We're going to talk," he said in his most authoritative voice. That tone had made more than one person back down and tremble.

She merely shrugged at him. "Whatever, Derek. Hurry up, then, so I can lie back down. What time is it, anyway?" she asked. She then turned toward her clock and gasped in outrage as she turned back on him. "It's freaking six-thirty in the morning," she yelled, as if she couldn't possibly believe he'd dare to approach her so early. "On my day off!"

This was her one weekend in who knew how long that Jacob was off with his friends and she could have slept at least a few more hours. She was so angry with Derek now that there was no way she was going to be able to get back to sleep.

She walked steadily toward him with a look so full of fury, he found himself retreating a step. But when he realized what he'd done, he stopped dead. He wasn't about to give ground, especially not now.

She got within inches of his face and poked her finger hard into his chest. "This had better be a life-or-death matter," she growled.

He was so unbelievably turned on he forgot about why he was there, or why they needed to talk. After the night he'd had, he couldn't believe his mind could wander. What the hell was wrong with him? What was this woman doing to his normally cool and collected self?

He grabbed her cup, which made her gasp again in fury and then set both of them on a nearby table. For the space of a few heart-pounding moments, they just stared at each other, her in a fury, him confused. Then, his will sunk and he pulled her into his arms and kissed her with the full force of the desire he'd been holding in the entire week.

She pummeled his chest for about two seconds, and then her body went limp in surrender. He was planning only to kiss her, to show her he was the one in control, but once his lips were connected with hers, he couldn't seem to stop himself. His hands ran down her back to grip her luscious behind and pull her up tight against his fully aroused body.

She gasped as her body connected with his, and she felt the arousal pressed into her core. She threw her arms around his neck and held on tight as he seemed to devour her whole. His hand continued to grip her, lifting her completely off the ground, and then he turned so her back was pressed up against the wall. He ground his hips against her, trying to relieve the intense pressure below his belt.

He wanted her, and if she came to her senses and told him to stop, he thought he might die on the spot. He was tangling his tongue with hers as his hands massaged her beautiful behind. She was so unbelievably curved in all the right places. Her backside was a perfect fit in his large hands, and it made him squeeze his fingers a little tighter. A growl of appreciation escaped her throat, sending Derek to a whole new level of wanting. Of desperation.

"Where's your room?" he asked before once again kissing her senseless. Unable to speak, she lifted her arm and pointed down the hallway. He took that as a yes and started heading in that direction, with her wrapped around his waist.

He reached an open doorway and her scent came in more strongly, drifting out so tantalizingly. He knew it was her room. He strode through the doorway and lay her down on the bed. After stripping his clothing away and then pressing down into her, he connected their lips once more before either of them could realize they were making a mistake.

He broke contact with her only long enough to pull the shirt over her head and yank off her shorts. He tossed them aside, not caring where they landed. He was finally stretched out against her fully, skin to skin, and his body was so on fire that it had to be burning her. He couldn't stop touching her; his hands roved from her beautiful breasts down her thighs and back up again.

He finally stopped kissing her, only to trail his lips down the smooth column of her throat. He licked along the pulse point, feeling his own skip a beat as he realized how quickly hers was pounding. She'd been passionate when they were young, but she was a wildcat as an adult. He reacquainted himself with all her curves, appreciating the way her body had matured.

In the office, he hadn't gotten to lie against her, hadn't gotten to see her sweet curves, and he was taking full advantage of relearning her body.

He brought his mouth down the mounds of her breasts and sucked in a tightened nipple. As he continued to massage it, she arched her back, reaching down to hold his head close to her body. He nipped at the swollen bud and then licked it. Another moan escaped from her throat.

He switched to the other side, giving her other breast equal attention, before continuing his journey down her body. He wanted to explore every single inch of her that he'd missed out on over the last ten years.

He reached her stomach and ran his tongue over the satin skin. When he got lower, near her core, he discovered a few little scars, which only added to her sexiness. He wondered briefly if they were from her pregnancy, but in his passion, he couldn't focus long enough to ask. She was the most beautiful woman he'd ever made love to. He was dangerously aroused, and he was unable to think about anything other than sinking deep inside her.

He finally reached her sweet womanhood and flicked his tongue over the swollen pink flesh. The taste of her made his erection pulse painfully.

He kissed her in the most intimate way a man can kiss a woman until she was writhing underneath him and moaning out his name, begging him for more. He slipped his fingers inside — she was more than ready for him, and he couldn't wait any longer. He moved quickly up her body and then locked his lips again with hers.

She greedily took everything he offered while rubbing her hands all over his taut muscles as she writhed to bring them closer. "Please, Derek," she cried out, "please. Now!"

He spread her legs apart and then rubbed his engorged member along her folds. The heat emanating from her was making him light-headed. She was so wet and hot, he couldn't play any longer. He grabbed her hips and thrust inside her in one quick motion. She cried out as he filled her up with his full length.

He paused for a moment. He wouldn't be able to give her pleasure if he didn't get himself under control. She jerked her hips in need, and he couldn't take any more. He started thrusting hard, in and out, while holding her hips tightly in his hands.

Their tongues continued to mimic their lovemaking, tangling and thrusting into each other's mouth, as they both groaned out their passion. He began driving into her harder and faster and gloated at the exquisite delight shooting through his body. He felt her body tense as she reached higher toward her release.

She gave forth a loud gasp, threw her head back into the bed and cried out as her body started convulsing around him. She gripped him tightly, deep within her, and he almost lost consciousness as his release shot deep inside her body. It felt like lightning zipping through him.

Her spasms still held both her and him in their grip, and his release was complete. It was the most intense orgasm he'd ever had in his life, and with his energy depleted, he fell against her sweat-slickened body. They both breathed in deep gasps of air.

He had to be crushing her, so with the last of his energy he turned their bodies so he was holding her tightly against him on their sides. They were still connected — he was unwilling to pull from her scorching heat. She wriggled — was she trying to get even closer to him, as if she couldn't let him go, either? Yes. Obviously.

They lay there for several minutes until their breathing slowed down and the flashing intensity of their lovemaking began to dim. He knew the moment she realized what she'd done — her body stiffened, and she began to push him away.

He reluctantly let her go. Her breaking of their connection made him somehow feel empty, and he couldn't understand why. With other women, he'd always been the first one to crawl out of bed and leave before they could possibly want anything as intimate and as tiresome as cuddling. That was for beforehand.

Was this what lovemaking really was?

Jasmine was staring at him with wide eyes filled with shock. She grabbed her sheet and covered herself up, and he felt more disappointment. He enjoyed looking at her body and wanted to continue to explore her. He hadn't gotten to map out her new curves nearly as much as he wanted.

"I...I...d...don't know why that keeps happening," she sputtered to him, as her cheeks filled with color.

"Because we have undeniable chemistry," he said with his trademark smile — the one that oozed overconfidence. He was feeling pretty good at that moment. He hadn't planned on starting his day out by ravishing her, but he could think of far worse things he could have been doing.

"I don't sleep with strangers," she blurted out.

"We're not strangers, Jasmine, so don't try that crap on me. You were a virgin the first time I took you, and, from the feel of your body, you haven't taken too many more lovers," he said. He was lying there in all his naked glory, and her eyes strayed south, where he was still at half-staff. She quickly snapped her gaze back to his face, and then her eyes narrowed as his grin became full-fledged.

She reached out her hand and slapped him hard once again before he had time to react. His smile disappeared, and he pounced on her before she could scramble away. The sheet slipped, and he held her down. His body was becoming, once again, fully aroused.

"I have allowed you to slap me twice now. It won't happen again," he growled before locking his lips with hers. She pressed her own together tightly and glared at him. He smiled, and then licked the swollen bottom lip. He pulled it into his mouth and began gently nipping at it. She gasped as the fire started building in her stomach again.

How had he turned all her rational thoughts to jelly with barely a touch? When he ran his tongue over hers again, as he held her hands up high above her head, she slowly opened to him, and when he put his tongue back into her mouth, she writhed. How could she help it?

Her stomach clenched. Still holding her hands together with one of his, he moved the sheet from her body as he ran his other hand down over all the contours of her body. She was soon desperate for him to love her again.

"Say you want me," he growled, with his impressive manhood pressed up against her core. Her body was on fire, and she wanted him deep within her, but she didn't want to utter those words of surrender. She shook her head *no*.

He continued to stroke her with his tongue and then inserted his fingers deep inside her moist heat. "Say it," he whispered in her ear, sending a shiver of delight down her spine.

She couldn't fight him anymore. She wanted him more than she wanted air. "I want you. Please," she finally begged. He removed his fingers and then slowly thrust back inside her, taking his time filling her. They'd been frantic and wild only moments before, but now he was gentle and loving.

Her body was quivering with need as he moved his impressive length in and out of her heat while continuing to kiss her lips, neck and breasts. She wanted more. She needed more. She was on the edge of a cliff, and only he could push her over.

She grabbed his hips and thrust up against him, groaning as the full width of him settled against her. "Please, Derek, faster. I need…" she gasped.

His eyes dilated at her gasped words. He picked up his speed until they were once again crying out in ecstasy.

When their passions were sated, he reversed their positions and held her close in his arms, unwilling to let her go.

She seemed to know she'd lost the battle and curled up against him. He was so depleted, he couldn't even open his eyes. He pulled the covers up over them and drifted off, feeling better than he ever had in his life. *He'd deal with the real world soon enough* was his last thought as he drifted into a deep slumber.

CHAPTER SEVENTEEN

MOM, I'M HOME!" Jacob's excited shouting woke Jasmine up from her deep sleep. She heard his running footsteps and then saw him peek in her door. "Yeah, she's here, Mrs. Winters. Thanks for the ride!"

After the boy spoke, the front door closed.

"Hi, Jacob," she said groggily. Then she glanced at the clock. She was shocked to see it was past eleven. A stirring next to her had Jasmine fully awake in an instant and more than fully distressed. For a moment, she'd thought the morning had all been a dream.

Her son's eyes widened as he stared at Derek. "Who are you?" Jacob asked.

Jasmine must have looked completely horrified. Her son had never once seen her in bed with a man; in fact, she hadn't been with anyone but Derek, ever. She looked over at her lover and, to her ever growing dismay, found his full attention on her son.

She wanted to jump from the bed and hide Jacob from

Derek's assessing eyes, but it was too late. She had no idea how she could get out of this. She couldn't believe she'd made love to the man in the house that she shared with her son — not only once, but twice. And then she'd actually fallen asleep in his arms when her son was due to be returning. It was just plain stupid, not to mention utterly irresponsible. She'd always felt nothing but contempt for people who allowed their children to see them in bed with their lovers. Her mind was scrambling to figure out how to explain her nine-year-old son.

Derek continued to stare at the boy — the reason for his initial visit slamming into him with the force of a two-ton wrecking ball. It was like looking at a picture of himself from his childhood, and he could have no doubts that the boy was his. How could he have forgotten — for even a single moment — why he'd come knocking on Jasmine's door at the crack of dawn?

Conflicting emotions warred inside him. Foremost, there was joy that he had a son, and yet he was enraged that Jasmine had kept his son from him. Confusion flowed through him, too — he had just had the best lovemaking of his life, and yet he wanted to strangle the mother of his child, the woman he'd just sunk deep inside before falling asleep with her in his arms.

Derek didn't know which emotion to embrace first. But his son had asked him who he was, and Jasmine was sitting there like a deer caught in the headlights of an onrushing car.

"I'm your dad," he said. He heard Jasmine's intake of breath and didn't even bother to look over at her. He was too afraid he might give in to his urge to throttle her.

"Really?" Jacob asked him skeptically, his eyes clouding as

if he didn't know whether to trust this man or not.

The boy's face twisted into such a mirror image of his own that Derek wanted to shout for joy. He was meeting his son. He wanted to jump from the bed and pull him into his arms, but he was still completely naked underneath the protection of the bedding. He knew Jasmine was still in the bed only for the same reason.

"I really am," Derek said, having to fight the emotions trying to break free as his throat closed up.

Jacob looked hopeful, as if he wanted to believe this stranger lying with him mom, but also as if he didn't want to be disappointed. Derek's heart thumped. What would happen next? Frightening his child wouldn't start their relationship off on the right footing.

"If you're my dad, then what did you say to my mom every night before you had to leave?" Jacob asked, and Derek knew he was being tested. Derek hadn't thought about those words in many years, and yet he'd never forget them.

He took a deep breath and uttered the words he hadn't said since the night before he was to meet Jasmine and run away. "Sweet dreams, my princess. I'll rescue you from the tower in the morning light." His throat had a slight scratchiness to it.

He heard Jasmine gasp again and then felt her body shake slightly. He glanced over at her and saw the tears falling. Why would she cry? Was she afraid now that her secret had been revealed? Would she have ever told him had he not come over? There were so many unanswered questions.

Before he was able to voice a single one, the breath was knocked from him as Jacob leaped onto the bed and threw his arms around him. Tremendous joy flowed through him as he held his son for the first time. He was awed and amazed by the little man. He wrapped Jacob up tightly in his grip and held the little body against his own. No hesitation.

"You're my dad," the boy said in awe. He lifted his hands up to touch Derek's face, as if he were trying to figure out for sure whether he was real. "Mom said you had to go away for business, but she told me that one day you'd come back, and you did. You really came back," Jacob said as a tear slipped from his eye.

Derek felt as if his heart had just burst in his chest. Jasmine was now sobbing next to them on the bed. She'd lied to Jacob, and lied to him by not saying a word.

Derek was afraid to look her way, unwilling to allow anger to dim the joy of this moment.

Jasmine watched as father and son embraced, and her world felt as if it were coming apart. Jacob had wanted a father for so long, but she'd done the right thing. She'd tried calling Derek that day he hadn't met her at the church — tried to find out what was happening.

He had been long gone with not a word to her when she'd found out she carried his child. And now, he'd been back in her life for only a week. How was she to know how he'd react to having a half-grown child? This was all too much. She needed a few moments to gather herself together.

In the span of a single week, her life, the one she'd built on her own, had come tumbling down, and reassembling the pieces and making it whole again appeared almost hopeless.

She had told her son all about Derek, though without

telling him Derek's actual identity, and she'd stressed the way he'd seemed like her knight in shining armor. She'd never told her son any of her heartbreak — how she'd waited for him in futility at that little run-down church. She had wanted her son to think his father would move heaven and earth to be with him, because that's how a father should feel.

Jacob was talking a million miles a minute, asking a ton of questions, and Derek patiently answered each one. They continued to cling to each other, and Jasmine felt like an intruder. She would have gotten up to give them some time together, but she was trapped underneath the covers and she didn't want to interrupt, didn't want to see the light dim in her child's eyes. He was so happy right at this moment. She scooted over, but her bed wasn't big, and Derek was a large guy. No matter how far she moved, they were still touching.

"Are you going to come to my wrestling match?" Jacob asked, hope shining in his eyes. "But if you don't want to, we can skip it."

The boy had never missed a meet. It broke her heart how much her young man wanted to please his father after just meeting him.

"Nothing would make me happier than to watch you wrestle," Derek said.

"It's really fun. Just ask Mom. She never misses my games. She always yells too loud, but Coach says it's OK 'cause she's just really proud of me," he said. "I kind of like it, though," he whispered to Derek, thinking she wouldn't be able to hear.

For the first time since her son had broken through her bedroom door, Jasmine felt the smallest tug at her lips as a smile wanted to form. Yes, she praised Jacob the loudest in the crowd. She'd been both mom and dad for nine years of his life.

"Can you go to the kitchen for a minute, so your mom and I can get ready to go?" Derek asked. Jasmine was relieved. She needed to get out of the bed.

"You promise you won't leave?" Jacob asked, looking as if he was on the verge of tears.

Derek grabbed him close again. "I promise you that I'll never leave again," he said, and then he glared at Jasmine over Jacob's shoulder.

A shiver ran down her spine. So he wasn't happy with her… She stiffened and glared back. She wasn't the one who'd walked out on him. How dare he look at her that way!

"OK, I'll be right out here," Jacob said, almost like a threat, in case Derek decided to disappear on him.

The boy slowly left the room, closing the door behind him. As soon as he left, Jasmine grabbed the sheet and jumped from the bed. She ran into the bathroom and locked the door. She needed a few minutes to collect herself before she had to face Derek. She leaned against the sink and took some deep breaths. A few seconds later, she heard Derek outside the door.

"You can either open this door or I'll break it down. It's your choice," he said in a voice of deadly calm. She waited a moment, trying to decide how important the door was. There was no doubt in her mind that Derek would break it. Reluctantly, she finally unlocked the knob.

He was standing there in nothing but his slacks. She said nothing for a few moments, not knowing how to begin this conversation. It was one she'd known would someday happen, but she'd assumed Jacob would be grown by then.

She decided to go on the offensive. "You didn't have to blurt that out to him. What if you're not his father?" she said, and then took a step back at the fury in his eyes. So much heat was coming from his eyes that she felt her face warm up.

"Don't even *try* to play games with me, Jasmine. It's more than obvious he's mine, and you have already robbed me of nine years of his life. You won't take anything else. Do I make myself clear?" He backed her into the corner.

She went from offensive to defensive in a matter of seconds. "I didn't say he wasn't yours. I just said you should have asked me first, instead of blurting it out like that."

"So you could come up with some more lies? I don't think so, Jasmine. Get yourself together. I'm going to spend the day with my son, and I'd rather he not know that I want to hurt his mother," he snapped at her before turning to leave.

"Now wait just a darn moment, you worthless bastard."

"What did you call me?"

"I think you heard me. Neither of us will win parent of the year or the decade, especially after Jacob caught us in bed that way. When you came here today, was it to find out whether my son had anything to do with you? Or was it so you could get a quick and easy lay? Obviously I rolled over fast enough, so my guess is the latter."

"*Our* son. And, yes, I did come to find out if he was mine." Derek looked at her levelly, ignoring the sex comment and focusing on Jacob.

Convenient now that he was all huffy and worried about being a dad. He hadn't been while lying on top of her.

"Wonderful. So you barrel into my house and instead of even asking about the boy, you jump my bones. I knew Jacob wasn't home, but you didn't, did you? In fact, you had every reason to think he'd be here asleep. But you gave him not a single thought once your 'other brain' leaped into action, did you?"

"So I got carried away. It seems to be what happens whenever we're together. That doesn't change the fact that you lied to me, Jasmine — took away nine years that I would have gladly wanted."

"Brilliant defense," Jasmine said with a snort. "That's probably what you told yourself when you took my virginity ten years ago."

"Look, lady, you wanted it as much as I did, even back then. And you definitely wanted it now." He threw her an offensively smug glance.

"You are insufferable. Still, you speak of sex with our son a couple rooms away. How can I take you seriously?" she snapped.

"Believe me, you'd better take me seriously, because I am beyond pissed off right now. I would have been there every day of my son's life."

"How in the hell would I know that, Derek? Seriously? You left me standing there like a fool — scattered to the far ends of the earth. I had no way to reach you, no way to tell you I was pregnant. How was I to know you'd want to be a father?"

"I'm going to do us both a favor and walk from this room. By no means does that mean that this discussion is over, it just means that I want to spend some time with my son, and

I really can't do that if I'm in prison for murder," he snarled.

"Threatening now, Derek? Really? That's who you are now. I guess I really didn't know you back then."

"They're just words, Jasmine. Quit twisting everything I'm saying," he sputtered, running his hands through his hair as he moved to the door.

"I don't know you, Derek!" she yelled, then calmed her voice. "I just don't know you." Sadness warred inside with anger as she gazed at the man who'd once been the boy she loved so very much.

"You could have known me. You chose not to because your greed got the better of you," he said, his eyes narrowing again, making her spine stiffen once more.

She had to restrain the impulse to slap the SOB for the third time. "Greed? I'm not a high-and-mighty billionaire like you, and I don't live in luxury, do I? Anyway, I had good reason to think that you'd dump me and my son like a hot potato once things got too scary for you. I wonder about back then, about your leaving. Did you decide you didn't want to dirty your middle-class hands with a millionaire's daughter?"

"You amaze me with your revisionist history. And with the words *revisionist history*, I mean bold-face lies. You know exactly what happened. And I'm too disgusted with you right now to stay in your presence any longer." Derek stormed out without another word.

CHAPTER EIGHTEEN

J ASMINE SLID DOWN to the floor and sat there, fighting the urge to sob out of anger and frustration. How was it that the vile excuse for a human being kept getting under her skin, kept affecting her even after she'd been away from him for nearly ten years? It didn't help knowing that she'd have a terrible time now getting rid of him. He was the one with all the money, all the power. What in heaven's name could she do to keep her life and herself together?

She finally got up and walked into the bathroom without bothering to lock the door. She climbed into the shower and stood there until the water turned cold. Then she reluctantly climbed out, shivering — so appropriate to what she was feeling.

She pulled on thick sweatpants and a sweatshirt, threw her hair in a ponytail, and didn't bother with makeup. She had little energy to care about her looks, even though she was going out in public. She was simply too frightened about what would happen next. She also knew she couldn't show that terror to

Derek, couldn't give him any weak spot to sink his fangs into.

She walked into the kitchen to the sound of her son's laughter. She smiled at him and kissed him on the head. To see such joy shining in his young eyes made the misery she was feeling almost worth it.

"Oh, Mom," he grumbled, and then he performed his patented eye roll for Derek. Jasmine held her breath because if Derek said that the boy was too old to have his mom kiss him in public — yes, how gross! — Jacob would never let her do it again. He was already in the throes of hero worship.

Derek surprised her by grabbing her around the waist, which knocked her off balance, so she tumbled into his lap. He kissed her squarely on the lips and then released her just as quickly. There wasn't even time for her to have a reaction to his audacity.

"Jacob, we never complain when a beautiful lady wants to kiss us," he said and then waggled his eyebrows at him. Jacob giggled, and Jasmine's heart thawed just the tiniest bit. Derek had said exactly the right thing — for now. Yes, he'd gotten one thing right, but that didn't mean he would make a great father, and it certainly didn't mean he'd earned the right to be a father.

"Yuck, Dad," Jacob said with more giggles, and then went back to scarfing down his breakfast. He looked up every few seconds to stare at Derek. Just checking.

"I need to make an after-match meal for the boys," Jasmine murmured, and she set to work making a large pot of chili and rolls.

The smells coming from the kitchen were making Derek's stomach growl. He was blown away with the speed with which she moved around. The meal was done in record time.

"Coach says Mom makes the best food ever, and that's why they always want her to make stuff for our tournaments."

"If it tastes as good as it smells, I can understand why your coach says that," Derek said.

Jasmine felt a little bit of pride roll through her. She enjoyed cooking for her son. Heck, she enjoyed cooking for anyone who appreciated it.

"Hurry up, Mom, or we're going to be late," Jacob called to her an hour later. She was putting the chili into the insulated bag. She had several things to drag out to the car and was feeling flustered, since she'd overslept and was officially running late.

"Let me grab those for you," Derek said, making her jump. She wasn't used to having someone there to help.

"Thank you," she muttered, relinquishing a few of the bags.

"We can take my car." Those words, if spoken by mere mortals, would be a suggestion, but from Derek, they were a command.

"Yesss," Jacob said, and then he gasped as he saw the shiny black car sitting at the curb. "Is that your car?"

"Yep," Derek replied with disgusting smugness. Jasmine just rolled her eyes at the rapture the two boys were sharing as they both admired the disgracefully expensive Porsche.

"My friends are going to think I'm so cool," Jacob said; he was bouncing in place at just the thought of riding in the fancy sports car. As Derek looked at his sleek sports car and then his son, he began to think it was time to upgrade to a bit more of a family-friendly vehicle. However, the excitement shining in Jacob's eyes had him eager for the ride to come.

"Want to take the top down?" Derek asked.

"Yeah!" Jacob shouted and then giggled as Derek pressed a button and the top started slowly moving back. Jasmine wasn't thrilled to climb into the small vehicle. She much preferred her sturdy minivan, which had a heck of a lot more metal around it for traveling the Seattle freeways.

Jacob climbed in the backseat and buckled up. It was a good thing he was still small, because he barely fit back there. No way could an adult squeeze in the back. She reluctantly climbed into the passenger side after storing her bags in the tiny trunk, and then when Derek sat down in the driver's seat, she was grateful the top was down. The little car was making her feel claustrophobic, and Derek was way too close for her already frayed nerves to handle.

Derek threw the car into gear and then pulled out on the street, picking up speed quickly when they hit the highway.

"We aren't in *that* big of a hurry," Jasmine gasped, and she held on tightly to the dashboard.

"Oh, Mom," Jacob groaned. "Go faster," he told Derek.

Derek ignored Jasmine's comment, making her teeth grind together in anger as he gave Jacob a huge smile in the rearview mirror and then jumped onto the freeway, gunning the engine.

They shot past cars at such a rate that the other people looked as if they were standing still. Jacob was full of laughter as his hair blew back in the wind and they flew down the road. Obviously, Derek wasn't a good father if he was putting their son in danger. She would talk to him once they were safely stopped — and he wouldn't like what she had to say.

They reached their exit and had to slow down, allowing

Jasmine to breathe.

"We've got to do this again," Jacob shouted from the backseat.

"We'll go on a long ride after the wrestling meet and then go have dinner," Derek said.

Jasmine didn't appreciate the way he was just assuming that she and Jacob didn't already have plans. She would have said something, but didn't want to get into a fight in front of her son. She couldn't wait to get that man alone!

They pulled up to the school and Jacob grabbed hold of Derek's hand. "Come on, Dad. I want you to meet my coach."

"Let me help your mom carry the food in, and then I can meet him," he answered. Though Derek seemed to be enjoying Jacob's excitement now, that didn't mean anything. Anyone could be patient and excited for a few hours with a child, but she'd see how he acted in a week, or even a month. That would be the true test of how much he really wanted to be a father.

They walked into the gym, with Jacob's small hand clasped in Derek's; she walked on the boy's other side. To the rest of the world, they would seem the perfect suburban family. She knew the truth, though. She knew a confrontation was coming, and she was trying to prepare herself for it.

Derek barely had time to set the food down at the eating area before Jacob dragged him off. He was so proud to show his father off to his coach and all his friends. She watched as he crossed the room and ran to Chuck.

Chuck looked up at them with surprise, and his brow wrinkled before he managed to paste a smile on his face and shake Derek's hand. She knew he had to be wondering what was going on, as she'd never mentioned Jacob's father before.

Jacob must have insisted that Derek sit with him in the player's section, unwilling to let his dad leave his side, because she saw Derek Titan, tycoon, kneel down and take a seat on the mats. She would have caught flies if they'd been buzzing around, her mouth was so wide open. She quickly shut it and helped get the food ready for the boys.

"Who is that complete hunk of man meat with your son?" asked one of the *very* single mothers as she edged up to Jasmine's side. "Please tell me he's your long-lost brother and single."

Jasmine felt instant jealousy. Marla, unlike her, was dressed in a skintight outfit, with her hair and makeup done to perfection.

How could she describe Derek? They weren't a couple and hadn't been for ten years. He was the father of her child, and he'd just made such hot love to her that she was surprised her sheets hadn't gone up in flames, but she didn't have any rights over him.

"He's Jacob's father," she said simply. She didn't know what else to add.

"Yummy. You haven't mentioned Jacob's father before. Does he live out of town?"

Too much interest.

"We just lost touch for some years, but I don't think he's going to want to be away from Jacob anymore," she said.

"I see," Marla said, and then snaked over to her son, who just happened to be near Derek. Jasmine watched as the woman actually pretended to trip and fall against Derek. What nerve! And he unbelievably held his arms out to catch her — how stupid can you get?

Jasmine could feel her anger escalating as Marla sat inappropriately close to Derek and the two of them chatted like long-lost friends. She wondered what the heck they found so amusing. Still, it was none of her business if he flirted with some trampy soccer — er, wrestling — mom. Hell, he could wrestle with Marla for all Jasmine cared. He could marry her and be one big happy family, as long as the man left her and Jacob alone.

She knew she sounded like a jealous ex-spouse — even in her own head — but he wasn't even trying to hide his flirtation with another woman when in the same room as the woman whose body he had ravished a few short hours ago. The man was a cad, and she was better off without him.

"So, that's Jacob's father, huh?" Chuck asked as he came up to the table.

Jasmine was hurt and angry, and she needed to feel good about herself, so she adopted very friendly body language with the poor coach.

"Yeah, he's been gone a long time and wants to reconnect with Jacob," she said. She didn't want everyone there to know all her business, and certainly didn't want to broadcast the detail that Derek had found out he was a father only that day.

"Jacob seems pretty happy about it," Chuck said, as they both glanced over at Jacob.

Derek was looking directly at her, and he didn't seem to be laughing anymore. Maybe it bothered him a bit to have to sit and watch her flirt. Good!

"Yeah, Jacob is really excited about it." She found herself giggling as she touched his arm. What was wrong with her? She was now acting like the vixen mother who had her hands all over Derek. She needed to get a grip on herself, not on another guy.

Chuck's eyes widened at her touch and he moved a bit closer. He really was a good-looking fellow. He was about the same height and weight as Derek, though not quite as muscled. She knew a lot of the moms had crushes on the boys' coach and had been flirting with him in hopes of a date, but he had seemed fixated on her for some time.

"What are you doing later tonight?" he asked, and she could see the wheels turning in his head. He was asking her out again, encouraged by her flirting. Damn, she really hadn't thought about that. Before she could think of an answer, Derek appeared and cut the conversation short.

"Sorry, Chuck. We're going to be in the city tonight." Derek wrapped an arm around her, letting Chuck and every other man in the room know she wasn't available. And here he'd been practically drooling in the other woman's lap not two seconds ago. Derek didn't appear to understand irony.

"Oh, I was just thinking about having a pizza party for the boys to celebrate the end of their season," Chuck said.

Jasmine was impressed by his quick cover-up; he must have planned a backup in case she turned him down again. Why had she used him to appease her own feelings? She was ashamed with herself. She shouldn't have let her temper get away from her like that, certainly not at the expense of a man whom she'd known as a good coach and man for the past two years.

"We should think about that for next weekend. I can order trophies for the boys if you give me a list of their names," Derek said.

"That would be very generous of you." Chuck's reply was sincere, though tinged with jealousy.

"It would be my pleasure. I've missed out on far too much of my son's life, and I plan on making up for that now by not spending another minute without him," Derek said.

"That's great. Well, I'd better get back over there and coach the boys." Chuck rushed off. He knew that Jasmine was off-limits and was making his quick escape.

She wanted to say something to Derek about his high-handed behavior, but she wouldn't give the nosy parents the satisfaction of a public fight.

Derek leaned down and kissed her intimately, an obvious move to mark his territory for everyone there to see. She knew it was a Tarzan thing to do, but she hoped it would make Marla back off. It wasn't that she cared if he dated someone else — OK, maybe she cared a bit — but she certainly didn't want it to be one of her neighbors.

As Derek made his way back to Jacob, she finally realized she was staring at the wretched man. But when she forced herself to turn away, she noticed that almost every pair of eyes in the building on her. She felt her cheeks grow warm.

She had to quit forgetting there was a world of people around her every time the man touched her. She busied herself with the food, plugging in the slow cooker and placing out the rolls next to the salads and desserts, stopping only when it was Jacob's turn to wrestle. She was no longer the loudest fan in the audience; Derek was encouraging Jacob throughout his match.

After Jacob won, he ran over to his dad, who lifted him up, spinning him around in a huge hug. She felt a tug at her heart as her son raced to her next and let her kiss him on the cheek and congratulate him. She loved him so deeply that there was nothing she wouldn't do to make his life better, even if it meant putting up with her insufferable ex.

The meet ended, and all the boys rushed to her table to scoop up the main course. She was pleased with all the oohs and aahs as the boys gulped down the chili as if it were their last meal. It didn't take long for every morsel to be consumed. Considering dinner was in only a couple more hours, she hoped they'd work up an appetite again by then.

She always stayed to help with the cleanup, and they weren't able to leave for about an hour. Most of the parents had gone home already, but she noticed Ms. Flirty Mom was still hanging around, along with a few other single women. Did they think that because there wasn't a ring on her left hand, he was still fair game? Or maybe she was just seeing something that wasn't there, all because of her own insecurities where Derek was concerned.

But again, why did she even care? He'd walked away from her and had been nothing but a bully since reentering her life. Let the women have him. She didn't want to play his games or be in his bed.

When they finally left the gym, she felt a little self-conscious as they approached his vehicle. This wasn't one of the more expensive schools in the Seattle area, one where cars like his were a normal occurrence. The attention they were drawing as they walked up to it wasn't at all pleasant.

"I'll see you all later," Jasmine said quietly to the few people left as she climbed in the ostentatious hunk of metal. She just wanted to get away from the women she'd once thought were her friends. She guessed friendship had a limit, and the impressive Derek Titan was over that limit.

"Thanks for all the help, ladies," Derek said with a friendly wave. "I guess I need to study up on wrestling so I'll know better what my son is doing."

Jasmine sat silently as they pulled away from the school. All she could think of was getting him alone for their talk.

And the long time it took them to return to her driveway didn't improve her mood.

She was the one who'd grown up the richest kid in town, whereas he'd been poor and worked for every dollar he made. Now the tables were turned. He was a billionaire, and she was the one barely getting by after her son's school tuition and her monthly bills. She didn't mind that so much — she'd never suffered from the obsession with class and income that had afflicted him in his youth and perhaps even now — but with his new status also came that arrogance and distance she didn't like. It was sad to see how a young man who'd once seemed so gentle and generous had changed.

They climbed from his car and walked into the house. Jacob could barely keep his eyes open, but he was fighting his exhaustion. She knew her son was afraid to go to sleep and then wake up to find his father gone. Though it was only early evening, the day had been exciting for her young son, who probably hadn't slept much the night before.

To send Derek away from her son now would be cruel. Jacob now had had a taste of being with his father. She wished that she could go back to the morning and that this time she'd be able to resist Derek's charms long enough to get him out of the house so she could think. She didn't want her son to be hurt.

"It's time for bed, baby. You can take your shower in the morning," she said.

"But I'm not tired, Mom." Right after he spoke, a huge yawn swallowed his features.

"That yawn says you're pretty tired, sweetie," she told him, leading him toward his bedroom.

"Will you still be here tomorrow?" Jacob asked Derek with big, sad eyes.

"I promise you, son, when you wake up in the morning, I'll be right here." Derek bent down and lifted Jacob up into his arms as if he weighed nothing.

"Will you read me my story tonight?" Jacob asked him.

Jasmine hated that the question made her jealous. Story time had always been theirs alone, and she didn't want to share it. The boy's next words suggested that he sensed her unhappiness. "If it's OK with mom, 'cause she always reads best."

It was something of a balm for her hurt feelings.

"I would love to," Derek replied.

"You come too, Mom," Jacob said, yawning again

"Of course, honey," she replied.

The three of them went to Jacob's room, which was filled with his favorite toys. Posters of Spider-Man covered the walls; the boy had been infatuated with the superhero for about a year, and in the obsession of youth and of an indulgent mother, he had every poster and action figure she'd been able to find.

"I really like your room," Derek told him.

"Thanks, Dad. Mom and me look for new stuff all the time."

"That sounds like fun," Derek said. "What story do you want to hear?" He looked over at the bookcase, which was crammed and overflowing.

"You can pick. I like them all," Jacob said as Jasmine helped him find his pajamas. He quickly changed and crawled into bed, sitting against the headboard. Jasmine leaned next to her son while Derek chose a book.

He found a superhero book and read the story, inserting villain's voices. When he made a pathetic attempt to imitate a damsel in distress, both Jacob and Jasmine burst out laughing. His inner woman wasn't at all in evidence.

"Hey, I thought that was pretty good," Derek said with a smile.

He finished the story, and Jasmine tucked the covers up under Jacob's chin.

"Good night, love. I'll see you in the morning." She turned to leave father and son alone for a moment.

"That's not what you say, Mom," he told her, and he waited expectantly.

She glanced at Derek self-consciously and then to her son, who was waiting. She whispered to him. "Goodnight, my young prince. May the dawning day bring you adventures, treasures, and so much more." With that, she quickly left the room.

She'd spoken the same words to him from the time he was a baby. It was one of her ways of giving him a piece of the romantic side of his father. She was very close to tears, since Derek was there, but he was no longer her Prince Charming. She'd fare much better if she remembered that.

Derek followed her into the living room a few minutes later, and they stood there, staring at each other. She knew it was time for the confrontation. It would just take everything inside of her not to explode and wake Jacob back up.

You must keep calm, she thought, but as Derek looked at her in his arrogant way, she knew it was much easier said than done.

CHAPTER NINETEEN

WHY WOULD YOU keep him from me?" Derek's eyes were filled with fury. What was worse than that, though, was the pain she saw under that anger. She'd hurt him without meaning to. But what did he expect of her? He had walked out on her when she was ready to give him her whole life.

"I didn't keep him from you on purpose — at first, at least. I had no idea where you were, and by the time I knew how to find you, it was simply too late. He was already walking and talking, and we were fine. The years just kept falling away."

"He's my son, Jasmine." He was almost shouting. "Were you going to tell me once we started working together?" She said nothing, but the look she gave him was all the answer he needed. "I see," he almost growled.

He began pacing the small room, and she felt like a mouse in the path of a viper. She knew he was going to strike, but she didn't know when, where, or how. All of the wrath that had been building in her all day was about to come unleashed.

"I'm so angry with you, I can't even think. I can't believe you could sit there with me each day, knowing it was one more day I didn't get with my son. I can't believe you would have sex with me and still feel no desire to tell me about him. How can you be this cold?" he spat at her.

"I…you…I don't know," she said, and she threw her hands in the air. "But why are you turning everything on me? Why aren't you taking any accountability for your own actions?"

"My actions?"

The outrage and bafflement in the question surprised her.

"Yes, your actions, Derek. I know that you're angry and frustrated now, but you have to admit that you were the one to walk away."

"Not that again! You don't expect me to listen to your twisted version, do you?"

"No, I guess I don't. I certainly wouldn't if I were you — I wouldn't want to be called on all your lies, your refusal to admit what happened." If he was angry and frustrated, she was starting to match him.

"Just can it, Jasmine, and answer me one thing. Did you know you were pregnant that last night — when we made all the plans?" he asked.

"Yes, all those plans," she said with contempt. "No, I didn't know until at least a month later. And what difference would it have made? Why would you have stuck around for a baby when you wouldn't stick around for me?"

"Yeah, right, I was the one who wouldn't stick around." Derek's voice shook. "Well, now I *am* sticking around, and you won't have a thing to say about it but *yes, sir*. I won't spend another day without him."

She knew that it was coming down to that.

"*Yes, sir*? Seriously? You expect me to just go along with your plans?" she asked incredulously.

"Oh, yes, Jasmine. If you want to still be his mother, you damn well will." His voice had grown eerily quiet and the hard truth in his eyes shook her to her very soul.

"Would you honestly fight me for him?" She was too much in shock to raise her voice. As he looked so coldly upon her, she felt her knees trembling and feared they would no longer support her, so she plopped down on the couch. She couldn't even look at him anymore, she was hurting so badly.

He stood there in the room — grim and wordless — but she refused to meet his gaze. His silence seemed to be the answer to her question. She knew he was going to fight her for Jacob. She had nine years of being his mother and had done the best possible job she could, but he had the money for the best attorneys. If he took her to court, he'd probably win. He'd at least get joint custody, stealing her son from her half the time.

It didn't help her case that Jacob was so desperate for a father that he'd bonded with Derek instantly. The courts always interviewed the children. They'd ask her son if he wanted to be with his father or his mother and, in his innocence, he'd tell them he wanted to be with both his parents.

They'd look at what each parent could provide, and Derek could win his share of custody hands down. She'd fight him the entire way, but she didn't have the limitless resources that were at his disposal. She felt defeated and devastated.

"I won't take you to court, Jasmine," he finally said, "but not because I give a damn what it would do to you. You don't deserve my consideration. The only reason I won't do it is that I refuse to hurt my son by pulling him away from his mother, whom he obviously loves."

Jasmine felt a ray of hope. She could handle weekend visits once a month. "Thank you," she said gratefully.

"I wasn't finished speaking," he said in a tone that had her snapping her head up to look at him. "I said I won't take Jacob from you, but I also told you I won't spend another day without him." He waited for his words to sink in.

Jasmine's eyes widened as she realized what he was saying. "You want us to live together?" she said in shock.

"I won't dishonor my son by just living with his mother. I will not allow the other kids to pick on him because his mother is a mistress."

"I don't understand," she began.

"Come on, Jasmine. You're smarter than this," She continued to look up at him blankly. "We're getting married. Get that, dear?"

Jasmine gasped and stared at him open-mouthed. He had just asked her to marry him. Scratch that — he'd just *told* her she was going to marry him. She didn't even know how to respond.

"I…I don't want to get married," she finally managed to stutter.

"That's very obvious from what you did ten years ago, but this isn't about you, or even about me. This is about Jacob, and about what's best for him, so you'll marry me because it's what's best for our son." Derek wasn't shouting or sneering anymore. He was calm as death and seemed almost defeated, which was worse for her because it made it all seem so much more real.

"What do you mean about ten years ago?" She just didn't understand.

"Stop stalling, Jasmine. There's no point in rehashing the past, especially with your creative views of it."

"OK, I'm tired of arguing with you; you've showed me in abundance today that you're hardly the most rational, or truthful, human being around." He rolled his eyes, but let her continue. "There should be a more reasonable solution than marriage. We can work out a visitation schedule." She was struggling to fix a situation that was quickly spiraling out of control.

"There's no other solution. I told you I want to be with my son every single day. I don't want to just visit him every other weekend and on alternative holidays. I've already lost half of his childhood. I won't lose anymore," he said.

"Can we at least take a few days to think about things and talk some more? This is all so new, and we are both too emotional." Perhaps if she tried to appease him, he'd calm down and start to see reason. Not that she was very hopeful.

"Jasmine, it's this…or else," he said, leaving the veiled threat unsaid.

She knew what the *or else* was, and it wasn't something she was willing to risk.

"I don't see that I have any other choice then," She refused to hide her resentment.

"Good. Now, don't think that there won't be an iron-clad

prenuptial agreement. When our son turns eighteen and goes off to college, our sham of a marriage will end, and then we can be free of each other. Don't worry, though, I'll leave you with something. Just think, while we're married, you get to live in the way you're so accustomed to. I may not have been good enough for you ten years ago, but I'm worth far more now than your father ever was."

"Not good enough for me ten years ago? You've got that wrong, because it's *now* that you're not good enough for me. I don't care about your money or what you can give me. I'm not the one wanting to get married anymore. I think we could and *should* find another solution." She let out a sigh of frustration. The more he lashed out at her, the angrier she got.

"I'm tired, Jasmine. I'm sleeping in the guest room." He rubbed his hand through his hair for the hundredth time.

Getting up to let him fend for himself, she dragged herself off to her room, feeling defeated and more drained than she ever had in her life.

Jasmine figured she'd climb into bed and lie there awake all night. Instead, her heavy eyes closed and oblivion quickly overtook her.

CHAPTER TWENTY

D AD!" JACOB CAME skidding into her room at the crack of dawn. This was beginning to be a pattern that she didn't like. Her first thought was *Why do I keep getting woken up so horribly early?* And then panic took over at the look of total devastation on her child's face.

"I knew he wouldn't be here." The tears were beginning to stream down Jacob's face. He crawled into the bed next to her to sob on her shoulder.

"It's OK, baby. He's here. He's just in the other room. He hasn't left." One of her own tears escaped at the poor child's unbearable heartbreak when he'd thought his father had gone.

"Hey, bud. Are you OK?" Derek stepped into the room and saw Jacob sobbing in Jasmine's arms. The boy looked up, and the tears stopped instantly; a watery grin spread over his face.

"You didn't leave!" Jacob exclaimed.

He jumped from the bed and threw his arms around his father. Derek picked him up and sat down with him on her bed. Jasmine scrambled up into a sitting position and pulled her legs up to her chest, hugging them tightly. Derek looked over at her with an expression that seemed to say, *I told you there was no other answer.* Sadly, she had to admit that he was probably right. For now.

"Where were you, then?" Jacob asked as he looked from his father to his mother.

"I was sleeping in the other room, bud," Derek said. As if that would satisfy him!

"But moms and dads sleep together. Maryanne says when her mom and dad stopped sleeping in the same bed, they stopped being married, and then her dad found a new person that Maryanne has to call Mom, even though she doesn't like her. She says she has to have two houses and doesn't get to be with her mom and dad together anymore."

It was the longest speech Jasmine had ever heard her son give. And Jacob's tears started to fall again as he thought about it.

"Your mom and I aren't going to live in separate houses, Jacob. We figured things out last night and decided neither of us could stand to be away from you. We'll stay together and be a real family."

"Do you promise?" Jacob asked with a hiccup.

"I promise you that," Derek replied. "As a matter of fact, you can be my best man when we get married."

"Really? Do I get to wear a tux...tux... Oh, I can't remember what they're called," Jacob said and blew his breath out with frustration.

"It's called a tuxedo, and if that's what you want to wear, then that's what we will wear. We'll have matching tuxes."

"And will Mom get to wear her princess dress?" Jacob asked.

"If she wants," Derek replied.

"Honey, I don't need to wear a princess dress. We're just having a small wedding, and I would look silly wearing a big, poufy dress," she said.

She knew they'd be married in front of a justice of the peace, and that was fitting in a ceremony without love. Still, she couldn't help but feel disappointed. She'd always dreamed that she'd have a wedding day from out of a fairy tale. She might still, since she'd be divorcing in nine years, but she seriously doubted it.

Too bad she'd learned long ago that fairy tales were just that — fairy tales.

"But, Mom… Hold on." Jacob jumped from the bed and ran out of the room. Jasmine looked at Derek and shrugged her shoulders.

Jacob came running back into the room, and she saw the familiar book about two seconds too late. She made a grab for it, but Jacob had already crawled back onto Derek's lap and opened the cover. Jasmine could feel her face flushing as Derek looked at a book that basically told him her dreams.

"Jacob, your dad doesn't want to look at that," she said as she tried to grab the book again.

"You do, don't you, Dad?"

"Of course I do, Jacob."

Jasmine clenched her teeth together and frowned up a storm. *He'd agree with anything Jacob said.* The kid could probably get a brand-new motorcycle from him if he just asked for it. She'd have to talk about that with him. And this was the last thing she wanted — to have her hopes and dreams laid out before the very man who'd broken her in two. She held the tears in as the two of them pored over her most private wishes.

"See, Dad, this is the dress mom wants to wear. She said that when she got married, it would be like a fairy-tale book, and she'd be the princess marrying her prince, and I got to be the young prince. She said she was going to find a frog one day and give him a kiss, and then he'd become her prince and rescue her from the castle tower. I guess that means you're the frog." Jacob broke out in giggles.

As Derek looked through the pages of the book, he knew he was intruding on her thoughts. But he couldn't stop looking. She had pictures and notes of everything she wanted for her dream wedding. He got to the back of the book and raised his eyebrows at her one more time. She'd even drawn pictures of what she wanted to wear on the honeymoon. She had excellent taste, and his mouth watered as he pictured her in a few of the outfits. Or without them. After he'd peeled them off.

"See, she has to have a fairy-tale princess wedding. She made me listen to a ton of those girlie princess books. She told me it was to teach me how to be the perfect prince for my own princess. I don't like girls, but Mom says that will change. I *really* think she's wrong, 'cause girls have cooties. It's OK if dads get married, though." Jacob had the look of one bestowing his greatest wisdom.

"We'll give your mom the fairy-tale wedding, then," Derek said. "You can help me to make sure everything is right, can't you?"

Jacob's eyes widened in awe as his father granted him that honor. "Of course."

"Good. Then that's all settled. Do you want breakfast?" Derek tucked the book under his arm.

"I can take that," Jasmine said, and she held out her hand.

Derek ignored her words and the look of fury on her face, and he walked out of the room with her book in his hand. If his son wanted his mother's dreams to come true, then that's what would happen.

His anger with Jasmine was still raging, but there was still something just beneath the surface that he couldn't explain. The girl who had stolen his heart was there, though he didn't want to feel that way. It would be hard to keep his heart hardened, but he needed to.

She'd crushed him one time, and that was enough — he wouldn't let her do it again. Still, he couldn't deny his need to give her the dream wedding.

Why?

He didn't know, and he refused to look too deeply. It was best to just retreat.

CHAPTER TWENTY-ONE

I KNOW YOU really like your house, or at least you say you do, but it's simply too small," Derek told Jasmine the next day while they were sharing a picnic in the park. "I'm going to contact an agent today and set up some appointments. I did a cursory look last night, and there are some really great places on the market I'd like to see. I'd prefer to build my own place, but it takes too much time, and I want us to get settled as soon as possible."

Jacob was playing soccer with some other kids, leaving Jasmine and Derek alone together for the first time that day. Her whole body tensed at his words. She liked her home. She knew it was small, but she'd been paying for it all on her own, and she didn't want to give it up.

"I don't want to sell my place." She'd crossed her arms and was glaring at him.

"You don't have to sell it. You can rent it out if you want or just let it sit empty. I can hire a cleaning crew to come in once a week to make sure it doesn't get moldy or damaged."

"I know what this is about. Once again, your insecurities about money are dictating what you do. My place just isn't good enough for you, is it?"

"*My* insecurities about money? You wrote the book. Sure, you're not living like the rich, spoiled little heiress you are — or used to be — but an obsession with money has always been behind everything you do. Especially with seeing that no one else but your family had it."

"And this is Mr. Billionaire talking, the regular guy with a babe-magnet sports car. You just can't handle the idea of a house like the one I live in now. It might reflect poorly on the size of your…wallet."

"Your house is fine, Jasmine, but…"

"But contempt was dripping off you from the moment you arrived," she snarled.

"I was simply amused by how the mighty had fallen. My offer of the cleaning crew stands."

"Once again, I don't really get a choice here, do I?" she snapped.

"I'm not your enemy, Jasmine. I'm trying to do the right thing for my son. How does my wanting to watch him grow make me the enemy?"

"Great. Make me sound like the bad guy. The next nine years of my life will seem like forever." How could she deal with a man like that, one who took what he wanted, when he wanted it? "Look, Derek. I've raised Jacob just fine on my own the last nine years. You won't come into our lives and completely disrupt everything I've built. I'm willing to make sacrifices, but you'll need to, as well." Her attempt at compromise left a bitter taste in her mouth.

"Fine. Can we call a truce for now, for the sake of our son?" he asked.

"What truce? You are the one saying what we are and aren't going to do. Doesn't a truce entail that I get some say in these matters? What if I don't want to move?" She refused to lose eye contact.

"So to be stubborn, to prove a point, you'll sacrifice what is best for Jacob?"

"I know what is best for my son, and I have done plenty of sacrificing for him. Don't always cast me as the villain!" she hissed.

"Then quit holding on to the past. You sure as hell don't want to let it go, or so it seems from where I stand. Is it so wrong to give my son a yard?"

"I have a yard." Sure, it was small, but it was still a yard.

"Why don't we ask Jacob if he wants a bigger house?" Derek was ready to call the boy over.

"Of course he'll want a bigger house. It seems all boys — young or *old* — do."

"Can we have one discussion without it turning into a battle?"

"When you can stop bossing me around."

Derek shocked her when he smiled. The expression in his eyes deflated her anger, and she hated to admit it, but she wouldn't mind a bit more space. It was just the way he was approaching the subject.

"Fine. I'll look at places, but I'm not promising anything," she said after a few moments.

Derek made a few calls while Jacob was playing, and within the hour he had appointments at six different locations. She was amazed at the speed with which that miserable man was able to get things done.

Jacob came running up to them and dived into the picnic fare.

"Hey, buddy. Want to go look at some houses?" Derek asked.

"Why?"

"We're going to find a bigger place to live so you have more room to play," Derek told him.

Jacob was very interested after that. He couldn't wait to leave the park and look at houses. The first few they went to left Jasmine in awe. She'd grown up in the biggest house in her hometown, but it didn't compare to the places they were inspecting now.

Each house had electronic gates, requiring a key code even to enter the driveway. The homes were enormous, and she was afraid she'd lose Jacob if they moved into one of them. One advantage, she supposed, was that she'd be able to hide away from Derek far more efficiently in a home this large.

Each time they left one of the places without leaping upon it, the real estate agent seemed disappointed, but Jasmine was impressed with how well she covered it up. Jasmine was sure the woman was going to make a killing off of the commission if she got it; as the price tags were in the millions.

The fourth house they went to had a similar gated drive and was just as big as the others, but it seemed different to Jasmine. It didn't seem as cold, as if the owners had actually lived in the home, not used it just as a museum. It was a colonial style that had a huge three-story entranceway done in white rock. The front door was big enough to drive a truck through, she thought.

"You said there are twenty acres, correct?" Derek asked the agent as they walked through the front doors into an impressive entry.

"Yes, plus a tennis court, full outdoor and indoor basketball courts, and an inside and outside pool."

"That seems a bit excessive doesn't it?" Jasmine said. She felt a lot out of her element. The place was nice, but it was just the three of them. It seemed ridiculous.

"Bigger is always better," the Realtor said without missing a beat. Jasmine's eyes unwillingly strayed to Derek's pants as she agreed with the woman with a secret smile on her face.

Derek looked up at her just as she lifted her eyes, and after covering the surprise in his gaze he sent a wink her way that made her blush.

No! This man was the enemy.

The Realtor kept on talking, either ignoring their small interplay, or just eager to make a sell.

When they entered the master bedroom, Jasmine felt as if she'd stepped into another house entirely. Never had she imagined a bedroom so large. Walking through a separate sitting room, they entered a large suite boasting two full-size walk-in closets with custom cabinets built in, and then, through another door, a master bathroom with its own Jacuzzi and separate walk-in shower and steam shower, as well as a sauna. The room also had its own private balcony with a gas fireplace, both in the room and on the covered balcony.

Wow. That was all. She didn't know what to say beyond that. She rather wished that the agent didn't know what to say either.

Quietly stepping from the room, the Realtor let them take their time looking around. Jasmine hated to admit it, but she was impressed. The home was palatial but it had a lot of touches that made it feel more like a home than a hotel, and she liked it more than any of the others. She just wished it weren't quite so large.

Was this a sign of Derek's past? Did he need this size of a home to prove he wasn't the boy from the wrong side of the tracks anymore? She couldn't tell. His face showed nothing as he looked around. Not pleasure, not disdain, just…boredom.

"Mom, I picked my room and it's so cool," Jacob said as he came running into the master suite. "It has a huge closet that's as big as my old bedroom, and I found a secret doorway that led somewhere. It was dark, and I couldn't find a switch and I didn't have my flashlight, so I couldn't go in, but I really like it, Mom. I could get so many more posters 'cause the walls are way tall." The boy was completely out of breath and beyond excited. Derek took one look at Jacob's face, and she could see that he had made his decision.

"This is the one we want," Derek said.

The real estate agent was virtually drooling on his shoes. She yanked out a stack of papers for him to fill out.

Derek decided to play macho man, Jasmine thought. "Since the sellers have already vacated the premises, I'd like to close next week," he told the agent. "We don't need a loan, so that won't be a problem. I'll have my assistant fill these out today and get them to your office Monday morning.

The Realtor was flustered. "I'll let them know, but what with all the necessary inspections and escrow, I'm not sure we can get everything done in that amount of time."

"I'll speak to my people, and there won't be a problem getting everything done. If the sellers agree to my offer, I can have this place ready to close in three days maximum," he said. The man had a way of speaking that made people want to jump to do his bidding.

Power.

It was total and complete power.

A shiver ran down Jasmine's spine as she realized she was going to be marrying him. She'd always have to remember who she was and not fade away behind his shadow. That might be all too easy to do.

"OK, Mr. Titan," the Realtor told him. "I'll get ahold of the selling agent — and hopefully the sellers — this afternoon. I'll notify you as soon as they have given a response."

"I appreciate it and will be *waiting*." Derek spoke as if he didn't like even to utter the word.

As Derek pulled up in front of her house, Jasmine thought it looked smaller than it ever had before. She squared her shoulders as she walked in the door. It might be able to fit into the living room of the other home, but she'd made it a great place for her little family, and there was nothing wrong with it.

Derek came up behind her and laid his hand on her shoulder. "Jasmine, I'm really not trying to put your home down. I just do a lot of business from home and need more space. Jacob will also need added security once the media realize he's my son. I have a lot of friends and even more enemies. That's the fallout of taking over companies for a living. I won't let something happen to him because some disgruntled person decides to hurt me through my child."

"I do understand," Jasmine said, though, honestly, she didn't really get it. She certainly didn't understand why everything had to move at the speed of light. But she didn't want to talk about it anymore, so she went off to her room to be alone. All the fight had left her for now.

Hopefully she found her fight again in the morning light.

CHAPTER TWENTY-TWO

O F COURSE, OF course. Everything always went the man's way. The house was his in record time.

When Derek offered to have a moving company box up her things, Jasmine put her foot down. Let a stranger to go through her belongings? Hardly! He actually had the gall to roll his eyes at her. He obviously thought she didn't have anything worth keeping. Maybe not to him, but they were *her* things, and she wanted to go through them all and sort them out.

She knew most of her furniture would end up being donated, and that was fine with her. The things she wanted to keep, she *was* keeping, and there was nothing he could do to stop her.

The next morning Jacob came rushing back into her room first thing. It had taken her a while, but she was starting to get used to the early intrusion. They all got ready together, and Derek insisted on using his car, telling her it was ridiculous to use two vehicles. She wearily went along with it; after all, Jacob was excited to be taken to school by both of his parents.

"I need to go by my place now and gather a few things," Derek told her. "There won't be time later before we have to pick Jacob up."

They pulled up to the luxury condominium complex and greeted the security guard at the front door. Jasmine was intimidated, as always, by the amount of money Derek had. She missed the boy who used to wear secondhand jeans and always had a smile on his face. This new man was so much more cynical about the world around him and took for granted things that the twenty-year-old would have been awed by.

They walked into his huge condo and, though it was nice, it was so cold. There was only one picture in the entire place, and it showed a much younger version of him with his arms slung around his two cousins. She remembered them well from when they were teenagers. They'd always been able to make her laugh. She smiled at the memories, remembering an easier time. Though they'd only had one year together, it had been the most carefree year of her life.

"How are your cousins doing?" She assumed that they were doing as well as he was because the three had been almost inseparable, and there was no way he wouldn't share his success with them.

"Both of them are thriving. I just saw Drew the other day, and Ryan is off in some other country right now. We all need to get together soon. It's been too long."

"They always made me laugh," she said, still gazing at the photograph.

"Yes, they both have a way of making people happy." He

packed up some clothing and then led her back down the elevator. They went out to the garage and, instead of getting back in the Porsche, he walked up to an SUV.

"I figure we should switch vehicles. The sports car is fun, but this has far more room for Jacob," he said. "Do you mind driving? I have work I could do on the commute."

He tossed her the keys. Just like that. And though he'd asked, there was no question in her mind that he expected the answer to be *yes*.

But because she wanted to drive it very badly, she didn't complain. She stepped inside and noticed there were hardly any miles at all on the odometer.

"You must have gotten this pretty recently," she remarked.

"I had it delivered yesterday. I figured we'd need it for Jacob, and my office manager said this was rated at the top for safety."

"You purchased a vehicle without even looking at it?"

"I trust my staff," he said simply, and then he buried his head in his laptop. Jasmine just shook her head at how truly different they were from one another. Money didn't concern him anymore, but when he was a teenager, he'd talked so much of his dreams and what he planned to do with his life. Times really changed, she thought sadly.

Ten years earlier he would have been looking at this car with awe, telling her all of his plans on how he planned on obtaining it — telling her he would move heaven and earth to give her everything she wanted.

Now, he was doing that, giving her what he assumed she wanted, but it wasn't out of love; it was out of some ridiculous need to show the world he'd arrived. At least, that's the way she felt about it.

She didn't know Derek, and though she desired him — that much was obvious — she didn't think she liked him much. Not much at all.

He hated her father; that was obvious. But did he know how much he acted like the man he considered his enemy?

She decided not to say that aloud. It would only start another fight, and she'd had her quota of fights for the week.

They arrived at the office and spent the first couple of hours going over the applications Jasmine had prescreened. Derek then had her spend the next few hours setting up interviews for the rest of the week. He said he wanted to get things settled quickly so the company could do as well as it should have been doing all along.

She wasn't happy about it, but she had to agree with him on a lot of things. Her father had hired some questionable people, and the company had been run into the ground. With a new staff in place, it was likely to do better than it ever had.

Now that they were moving farther away, it was going to be even less fun to come into this building, a building that brought up so many bad memories, reminded her so much of the father who had abandoned her, betrayed both her and her son.

She was thankful when the end of the day finally arrived and Derek actually didn't complain when she said it was time to leave.

In fact, what he said stunned her. She was ready for a real fight when she tried to explain the way she liked to do business.

"Derek, when Jacob isn't doing sports, he gets out of school earlier. I was able to take some of my work home with me before so I didn't have to put him in day care. I know you run your businesses differently, but I really do work well from home and would like to continue doing that." But she was so sure about what was coming. He was going to go off on her about her not being the owner's daughter anymore and not being entitled to special favors.

Not quite. "You can quit altogether, if you'd like. Of course, our son comes first, and there's no need for you to work," he told her.

"I don't want to quit." Jasmine stood there with her arms across her chest. "It's important for me to make my own money. Just because you have more than any small nation of people needs doesn't mean I'd ever be comfortable spending it. If you don't want me to work here, I can begin searching for other work." She didn't mention she'd already begun the job search.

"I didn't say I wanted to fire you. I just suggested that you might want to spend more time with our son. He will be grown before you know it, and I don't want you filled with regrets," he said, exasperated.

"And what about you? Are you going to stop work to be with him, too? It's not as if you need to work, either, and I wouldn't want *you* filled with regrets."

"All right, maybe I said that wrong. I love what I do. I get up in the morning and love going to work. The thrill of it, the chase of a good deal. I just think everyone should have that same feeling when working. If you want to work from home, we'll set up an office space there for you. If you want to come to the office, we can do that. If you want to find other employment, that is OK, too. I'm not trying to be an ass, here — for once."

Jasmine's jaw dropped a bit. OK, that was more like it.

She felt a tightening in her chest at the thought of having more time with Jacob. She really would like to be able to go to the school more often. She'd always been slightly jealous of those room moms helping at the school during the week with their kids. She spent plenty of time with her son and was there for all of his special events, but Derek was right that she was also missing out on a lot. So was he.

But would Jacob be better off if one or both of them sacrificed their own satisfaction and ambitions to their child? The boy was doing so well as things were. It was a difficult matter to consider.

"I'll work from home once we get moved. At least until I figure out what I want to do," she said, and the topic dropped. They left the building with a minor truce established.

Jacob came running as they pulled up outside the school, and he looked around with an eager expression on his face. He looked right past the SUV, so she stepped out and called to him. He walked over, with his eyebrows puckered, disappointed the Porsche wasn't there. But he shrugged it off and climbed inside.

They stopped by a moving company and loaded the SUV with empty boxes, picked up some takeout, and headed toward her house. The three of them carried in all the boxes, and the two men went into her son's room to begin the massive job of packing his belongings while she figured out what to do with the rest of the house.

After half an hour, she stood in the doorway and watched Derek and Jacob silently for several minutes, enjoying the sound of their laughter. They had bonded so closely in only a few short days and she was glad for that. They paused in their packing, and Derek tackled Jacob on the bed and tickled him until tears were falling from the boy's eyes, he was laughing so hard.

Jasmine reluctantly walked away from the room and headed into the kitchen. She put together several boxes and started deciding what she'd keep and what she'd donate. She knew a lot of her belongings wouldn't fit in with the new home, so the donation pile seemed to get bigger, while her packed boxes weren't taking up much room.

Derek came out every once in a while and hauled her boxes out to the garage, where he was making a nice pile for later.

There were certain things she wasn't willing to part with, such as her countless number of books and her mother's antique china, but there were many items she let go of with no qualms. By the end of the night, she was exhausted and had barely made a dent in the contents of her small home.

"Derek, there's no way I'll finish all of this in time if I'm working all day. I'm going to need to take the rest of the week off to get it done. When it's over, we'll set up my home office." She sat down on the couch, completely exhausted.

"I was thinking the same thing. We really just have a bunch of interviews this week, anyway. Take it off and get everything done. I'll get it all set up tomorrow and take the rest of the week off, too. This is a lot more work than I thought." He sounded just as tired as she was.

"Been a while since you did manual labor?" It was so tempting to goad him.

Derek looked at her with a wrinkle between his eyebrows. "Are you calling me a wimp?"

"Well…" she said with a tired smile.

"Fine, I'll give you that one." He chuckled and leaned his head against the back of the couch.

Jasmine chalked one up for herself. She hauled her exhausted body to her room and fell to her bed fully clothed and not even caring.

CHAPTER TWENTY-THREE

TIME FLIES WHEN you're not having fun.

During her week off work, Jasmine made impressive strides with her packing and had trucks from the local charity stop by twice because the items she'd decided to jettison had piled up and were filling her living room. It was a little disheartening to watch ten years of accumulation dwindle so dramatically and to see the home she loved become empty and almost foreign, but at least she could find some satisfaction in getting it all done.

On Friday morning, Derek was signing the final papers, and the movers were coming to pick up her things at noon.

Jasmine walked slowly around her once homey place and couldn't stop the tears from streaking down her cheeks. This home had been the first sense of real security for her little family. She had been so proud when she signed her name on those papers and knew the place was hers and no one could take it from her, not as long as she paid the mortgage, and now she was walking away from it. She felt as if she were abandoning her safe house.

Now everything was in boxes — or gone — and she was off to a new adventure. She wiped the tears away and decided to sell the place. The thought of returning to this home all by herself was too depressing even to contemplate. She'd walk through the rooms and see Jacob in every corner, and now she'd picture Derek's massive presence there, too. It would break her heart a little when someone else occupied it, but at least then it would be loved, and new memories could be created.

She composed her features just in time, because Derek stepped through the doors and took a look around.

"I guess there really isn't anything left to do but wait for the movers," he said. "I brought lunch, so let's eat, and I'll call the company and have them arrive here early."

The movers had the contents of the house loaded into the truck within a couple of hours and soon were on the road. Her place was empty, completely empty. Derek waited for Jasmine as she looked around with a sense of awe and regret. She looked in every cupboard twice just to make sure she hadn't forgotten a single thing and to lengthen her final moments in the home she'd loved.

To his credit, Derek didn't say a word as she dragged her feet. He even stepped outside to give her a few more minutes alone. One last tear slipped from her eye. Then she squared her shoulders, dried her face, and walked out the front door, shutting it firmly behind her as she said goodbye to her old life.

"Are you OK?" Derek asked her as they walked to their

vehicles. It was a rare and tender moment and almost started her tears right back up. Still, it wasn't as if he could understand why it was hard for her to leave. He'd had no problem leaving his old life behind. That thought still hurt, even after all these years.

"I'm fine. Saying goodbye to this house is just a little harder than I thought it would be. I know it's not much, but it has been home for almost nine years," she said with a little sniffle.

"It's a great place, and you kept it beautiful." He spoke a bit awkwardly.

"Thank you, Derek. I appreciate it, although I know you didn't really like my house," she said with a slight roll of her eyes. *Oh, no! I'm picking up bad habits from my son!*

"I can always have movers come and bring it to the property if you want. There's plenty of room," he told her.

She looked at him with her mouth hanging open in astonishment. She could tell he was completely serious. If she asked him, he'd actually pay the ridiculous price to have her home moved, just to make her stop crying.

She started to giggle at the thought. Didn't people move houses primarily when they were of historic value? They didn't move a silly little home just because a person felt attached to it. She laughed even harder when she thought about how much money the guy spent in a single day. It was probably more than she'd spent in Jacob's entire life.

"Thank you for the laugh, Derek. I'm feeling so much better now," she said and then, on complete impulse, threw her arms around his neck and gave him a hug. She hadn't initiated contact with him once since they'd reunited, and for a moment he stiffened in shock and then wrapped his arms around her.

She needed the comfort, though he was the one who'd also caused the pain. But still, she couldn't seem to draw back. Derek rubbed along her back and, even though he was the reason her life was changing so drastically, his comforting hands were making her feel better. She'd think about the irony later.

His caresses stopped being merely sympathetic. He started pulling her even closer to him, and his hand roamed lower with each pass. Her breathing deepened as his touch ignited bold fires in her body. He brought one hand up to her chin, lifting it. Before she had time to blink, he brought his lips down on hers in a sweet and drugging kiss. If he'd been urgent, as he normally was, she might have been able to resist him, but with this gentle side of him, she had no chance.

She leaned in as he deepened the kiss, making her stomach quiver with need. She couldn't help enjoying the feel of being held and the taste of him as his tongue slipped inside. She couldn't seem to get close enough.

"I didn't know you were leaving," a voice said, bringing her back to reality. Jasmine pulled back from Derek, who looked a little shaken up, and she turned toward the sound, to find her elderly neighbor standing a few feet from her. Either the woman was oblivious to the embrace, or she didn't care. She seemed totally unconcerned that she'd interrupted their passionate clinch.

"Yes, Mary. It's all happened so fast that I haven't spoken to anyone about it," Jasmine told her neighbor, feeling a little guilty about moving without saying goodbye.

"Well, we'll sure miss you and precious little Jacob," the woman replied.

"I'll miss you, too, and your wonderful peanut butter cookies." Jasmine's voice had a little hitch in it. She walked over and gave her neighbor a hug and then said her goodbyes.

"You can follow me," Derek said to Jasmine as he climbed into his vehicle.

She got into her own reliable minivan — which, sadly, held little appeal to her anymore after she'd driven his luxury SUV — and started off out of the driveway. She looked into her rearview mirror until her home fell out of view, and then let out a deep sigh.

When they pulled up to the new house, Derek entered the code for the gate to open. She drove up the long driveway behind him, taking in everything. She'd been there only the one time, and she looked at the place with new eyes, trying to drink it all in.

The home was certainly a show place. The lawns were immaculately manicured, though surprisingly lacking in flowers, and she vowed to change that as soon as possible. The driveway wrapped around a beautiful fountain. The property was both stately and yet with touches of home at the same time. She could grow to love the place — that is, if she could figure out how to get from one end to the other.

She had to park in the driveway, as there were two huge moving vans backed up to the massive garage. There were several men hauling items from the backs of the trucks and trudging into the house. She and Derek walked in together, and Jasmine was struck by how different the place looked with the walls bare and the furniture gone. There were a few pieces of his furniture from Derek's condo, but his old place had been much smaller, and they were going to have to buy a lot more pieces to fill the place up.

The house looked better to her, though, with all the previous owners' items out. She could now picture her own belongings filling up the spaces. The more she walked around the empty house, the happier she felt. She wished she could use one of the swimming pools to help work off some of her excess energy, but the pools wouldn't be available for use until the next day. Though they'd looked spotless to her, Derek had people in to perform a special cleaning because their son would be swimming in them.

"I've always had fantasies about sex in a pool cabana."

Jasmine jumped as she spun around to find Derek standing next to her by the pool. She'd felt so overwhelmed that she'd come outside to try to regroup.

"Well, you can keep fantasizing," she said as she tried to brush past him. His arm snaked out and pulled her against him.

"I was greatly disappointed to be interrupted earlier. I thought we might continue now," he said as he leaned down.

Jasmine lifted her hand and stopped him. "You can stay disappointed," she told him, though her heart rate had kicked up a few paces.

"Why be disappointed when we're here? The new home needs a proper christening," he said as he grasped her hand before gently grazing her lips. He nibbled on her bottom lip, sending fire through her blood.

"Derek…" she warned, though her mind was muddled and she didn't know what she was going to say next.

"Why fight this, Jasmine? We obviously have no problem in this department," he said as his hand tightened on her back and lowered over her curves.

She began to shake.

"Because…" Why couldn't she complete these simple thoughts?

She'd gone without sex for so many years — no problem — but now her body seemed to be on permanent go mode, and all it took was a single touch and she was ready to find a bed. Whatever happened to her willpower?

Derek said nothing; he just let go of her hand and crushed their bodies together, possessing her lips in a kiss of hunger.

To hell with it, Jasmine thought, and she wound her hands behind his neck, silently pleading temporary insanity in so far as she could think at all.

"Um, Mr. Titan…I'm…um…sorry to interrupt, but we need to have some papers signed."

Derek lifted his head and glared at the man. That was twice in a couple of hours' time. Tonight there wouldn't be any interruptions. At least, for the sake of his body, he hoped not. Leaving Jasmine standing there, he followed the man back into the house.

It took the movers only a few hours to get the trucks unloaded, and then Derek and Jasmine were alone in the huge place for the first time. She headed straight for the kitchen, more excited about that room than any other — OK, besides the library — and started to unpack boxes.

Derek had tried to persuade her to let the movers unpack, but part of the excitement of moving was to find her treasures and place them where she wanted. She didn't want strangers to do it. Besides, she knew she'd never be able to find anything if she didn't do it herself. Her kitchen had been one area in her old house that she'd splurged on. And the items that Derek had brought were pretty fantastic. It was fun sorting through his kitchen boxes, almost like Christmas.

"I'm going to pick up Jacob," Derek told her. "We'll be back soon."

Jasmine glanced up at the clock in surprise. How had it gotten so late?

"I can go with you," she offered reluctantly, and the smile on his face showed he knew what she was feeling.

"Go ahead and continue what you're doing. It looks like you're enjoying yourself," he said, and he turned to head out.

"Oh, look," she exclaimed. "There are lazy Susans in all the corner cabinets." Derek was forgotten.

She missed the smile playing with his jaw before he walked from the room, leaving her to explore all the nooks and crannies of her new kitchen. Yes, she thought of him as a monster, but he did want to make this work, and he'd do whatever it took to make that happen.

Derek was actually warmed by her love of the smaller things in life. She found excitement in lazy Susans, but frowned over the size of the house. Just when he began to think he had her figured out, she did something else that left him feeling as if something were tugging at his heart.

It was inconvenient. This wasn't a love match and he'd do

best to remember that.

He'd fallen so hard for her when he was a teenager because, even though she was the wealthiest kid in town, she'd never lorded it over anyone — unlike her father. She'd always preferred a pair of worn jeans and a T-shirt to the latest styles. She'd seemed far more like him than like the other rich kids in town.

If he looked at her home, vehicle and possessions, it seemed that not much had changed. What she owned was well kept, but nothing screamed extravagance. As a matter of fact, her son had far more possessions in his small room than she did, and that she loved and spoiled Jacob was abundantly obvious. He also knew how much salary she made, and it was ridiculously low for the job she did. Her own father hadn't given her a raise the entire time she'd been at the company. Derek had assumed that was all just on the books, that her dad was supplementing her income on the side, but, from the way she lived, he no longer believed that.

Had he been wrong? Maybe she wasn't the cold, materialistic person he'd thought her to be when she sent her dad to say her goodbyes. Maybe there was another reason the whole thing had happened. No, that made no sense. She'd betrayed his father and filled her dad in on everything, and the bank called back the loan it had promised Daniel to open his computer store. There was little point in asking her for her reasons behind it all. It wouldn't do them any good to keep rehashing the past.

When Derek reached the school, Jacob was out on the curb and jumped into the vehicle almost before he had it stopped.

The boy was talking up a blue streak — heck, this streak was bright purple — and couldn't contain his excitement about going to the new house.

Jacob asked whether all his things had arrived yet and if the pools were ready to swim in. He wanted to know if Derek had gotten him a basketball and if they could adopt a new puppy. Derek answered every question he could, but he didn't know whether Jacob even heard him — his son would fire another one off before he'd been given the answer to the one before.

The SUV was barely parked in the garage when Jacob leaped from the vehicle and dashed through the door. Derek heard the boy yelling a greeting to his mother before the footsteps faded away up the stairs.

"I hope he doesn't get lost," Jasmine said as she stared at the tornado of energy her son had just left behind.

"Well, then, we could play a land version of Marco Polo," Derek replied with a laugh. She stared at him for a moment and then caved in and let amusement take over. "I'll make sure he found his room and then see what I can do to get the place straightened up," he said and disappeared.

Jasmine didn't see either of the boys for a couple of hours. They all got lost in their different projects and in the joys of new beginnings.

CHAPTER TWENTY-FOUR

"**W**ELL, LOOK WHO'S coming up in the world," Drew said into the speaker as he waited for the gate to be opened. He wasn't surprised his cousins had found him in the new place, even though they had been in town only two days. They were actually a day late.

"How did you find me? I thought I was hiding," Derek replied. He'd been wondering who was buzzing him.

"Oh, it's always easy to find my prey," Drew replied.

Ryan's voice rang out over the intercom: "Hey! Open up this gate before I climb over it and kick your sorry butt."

"What the heck did you bring *him* for?" Derek said as he plunked in the combination for the gate to open. He walked out the front door and waited for his cousins to make it down the long driveway and emerge from the truck.

"Nice place. Got an extra room?" Ryan said as he came up the front steps and slapped Derek on the back.

"Sure. I do need to hire a gardener," Derek replied, which earned him another punch.

"Heck, someone is growing up to be a real boy. You got the house, the kid and soon a wife. Whatever happened to our vows of being bachelors forever?" Drew said as walked through the double doors.

"That was when we were twelve," Derek reminded him.

"Damn, I don't think you have enough room," Ryan called out with a low whistle.

"Whatever, Ryan. Your net worth is equal to, if not greater than, mine," Derek replied with a roll of his eyes.

"Well, yeah, it's more than yours now because I haven't spent it all on one house," the man replied with an evil grin. He knew the money spent on the house hadn't made the tiniest dent in what Derek had.

They made their way out to the back, drawn by the sound of Jacob splashing in the water. The boy spotted the two men, and his eyes filled with curiosity. Derek introduced them to Jacob as the boy's uncles — they were basically his brothers, after all. Jacob was ecstatic to find he had uncles, since his mom was an only child, and he had little family.

"I hope you have extra swim trunks because I'm getting in that water one way or the other, and I don't want to make you look bad in front of your fiancée by showing her how lacking you are," Drew said with a waggle of his eyebrows.

This time Derek punched him in the arm and then directed him to the changing area next to the pool. It was already stacked with extra suits. His two cousins changed quickly, and soon the four boys were having a splashing war that had Jacob giggling uncontrollably.

"So, where is Jasmine?" Ryan said, a slight tension in his

voice. At one time both Ryan and Drew had adored Jasmine, but with Ryan knowing about her betrayal, he didn't seem all that thrilled that she was back.

"Careful, Ryan. She's about to be my wife," Derek warned.

"I get that. I'd do the same. However…" He left the words unspoken.

"Maybe it's just time to let go of the past," Drew said, always the easiest going of all of them.

"Maybe it's not your business," Ryan said, climbing from the pool. Luckily, Jacob didn't overhear any of this.

"I just put family first. What she did was… Well, dammit, it really sucked."

"Look, I don't want to fight about this. I'm marrying Jasmine. I've had to let go of the past, and I think you need to, as well. For the sake of my son," Derek said, sending a pointed look toward Jacob, who was now returning from the bathroom.

"You know I will always have your back," Ryan said, clapping Derek on the shoulder.

The men got dried off as they went in to change.

"You never did say where she was," Drew said, pointing out the obvious, that she wasn't there.

"She had to go pick up some groceries so we could eat. Jacob here is a bottomless pit. Apparently he doesn't like grocery shopping, though," Derek said. "A chip off the old block. We're going to have to hire people to take care of the drudgery."

After changing, Drew and Ryan helped Derek get things unpacked. There was a floor-to-ceiling library that Jasmine had almost cried over. Derek wanted to surprise her by getting all her books loaded up onto it. Her collection was vast, but didn't even come close to filling the room up. The room was impressive and welcoming, with a wood fireplace and a huge window with a seat in it. They were going to spend the week shopping for furniture to fill this room, along with many others.

With his cousins there helping him, they had the library and living room unpacked in no time. They even managed to get most of the artwork hung on the walls, and they'd hadn't done a bad job, if he did say so himself. He looked around, thoroughly pleased with their progress.

They'd just sat down when he heard the garage door open. He stood up to help Jasmine carry in the groceries, and Drew and Ryan followed him.

When they stepped out into the garage, Jasmine saw them, and her entire face lit up. "Drew! Ryan! It's so good to see you," she said as she ran toward them, excitement evident.

"Jasmine, you're looking more gorgeous than ever. Are you sure you want to stay with this bum? I think I can convince him the kid's mine, and we can run away together," Drew offered her with a sly grin directed toward his cousin. His pleasure in seeing Jasmine was obvious. It was just as obvious that Ryan was a lot more reserved, though he gave her a stiff hug that she obviously noticed and backed off.

"Drew, I have missed your sense of humor," she said, directing her attention toward him. "You have to tell me everything you've been up to for the last ten years. I'm sure you've left a trail of heartbroken women in your wake."

"Yeah, Drew is just a barrel of laughs," Derek said, unhappy that Jasmine was so open and easy with Drew and so withdrawn when she was with him.

The guys grabbed groceries and set them on the counter so she could get them put away. They sat on the counters so they could continue talking to her while she put items where they belonged and then began making dinner.

The kitchen was soon filled with spectacular smells, and though a bit of tension accompanied the easy banter she shared with Drew, she did her best to brush it off, finally pushing the men out of the kitchen because they wouldn't quit picking at things and disrupting her cooking. It also made it easier to breathe when she didn't feel Ryan's eyes following her every movement.

What had she done to him? She didn't know.

When she finished making a salad and had the casserole in the oven, she decided to go work on the library. She couldn't wait until the day the shelves were filled from top to bottom. It would take many years, but part of the fun was going to be adding new additions to it each week.

She walked in the room and gasped. The guys had unpacked everything. Nothing was in the right place, but they'd tried. It warmed her heart to see that Derek had attempted to do something special for her. As she walked back into the living room, she saw his priceless artwork hung on the walls. The man definitely had good taste.

She felt they'd be able to decorate the house agreeably if what he had now was any indication. There were only a few paintings, but they were gorgeous, and she looked forward to getting more. Entering the sitting room, she walked up and gave Derek a hug.

"Thank you for putting all the books up. I know it must've been a bit of a pain, since I have so many of them," she said, not mentioning he'd done it incorrectly. It was the thought that counted.

"You're welcome. I wanted you to start feeling at home. I know this house is a little intimidating," he said with a shrug.

"It was very sweet of you."

"Hey, we helped too. Where're our hugs?" Drew said with a wicked grin. She went over and hugged him, not looking over at Ryan. She would need to speak to him, find out what the cold shoulder was about, but she didn't have the energy right now. Not after all the tension she'd been dealing with between her and Derek.

"I can't wait to go shopping at all the used bookstores and fill the rest of the shelves up," she said eagerly.

"I bet you have them filled up within a week, and then will have us over here building you more shelves," Drew said.

Jasmine had always been an avid reader in school. She never went anywhere without at least one book in her bag, just in case she ended up stuck in a line somewhere or on the Metro. If she had a book, she had a constant form of entertainment. She had an electronic reader, but it didn't offer the same sensual feeling as having a paper book in her hand did.

"I can't wait to get one of those super-cushiony couches so I can go in there and fall asleep with a good book," she said a bit dreamily.

"Oh, Cuz. It looks like you're getting replaced by a good couch and some fancy book hero," Drew teased him.

"You're both about to be booted out without dinner," Derek growled. But both men knew he was all talk.

The timer on the oven went off, and the men immediately headed for the dining room. Luckily, Derek had a huge table already, and there was plenty of room for all of them. She had the men carry the dishes to the table and then watched in amazement as everything she'd made disappeared in no time at all.

"This is good, Mom," Jacob said. The men quickly agreed with him in between bites.

Jasmine was feeling good, very good. The kitchen was a dream to cook in, and her company had enjoyed her meal.

"So, what's happened with your life since you left Derek in your wake and started over?" Ryan asked, sipping his beer as if he hadn't just completely insulted her.

CHAPTER TWENTY-FIVE

J ASMINE FROZE, LOSING all appetite as she looked at a much more hardened Ryan than the young boy she'd known ten years earlier.

Ouch.

"Ryan," Derek warned. Jacob kept on eating, unaware of the tension, since Ryan had spoken conversationally.

"I don't understand," Jasmine finally said, looking Ryan directly in the eyes. "What exactly is your problem?" If he wanted a showdown, he was damn well going to get it.

"I don't like anyone hurting my family," Ryan said, not backing down.

"Hey, buddy. Do you want to show me your room?" Drew asked Jacob, who looked up eagerly as he shoveled in a few more bites before jumping up.

"Sure. I have all kinds of Spider-Man stuff." The boy led Drew away, leaving Jasmine, Derek and Ryan at the now silent table.

"OK, Ryan, you have got to back off," Derek said as he

glared at his cousin.

"I know why you have to marry her. I get that. I would do the same for my kid. But she stole nine years from you. Doesn't that make you the least upset?" Ryan asked, more perplexed than anything.

"I stole nine years?" Jasmine snapped. "He was gone, Ryan. Don't you think he gets some blame in this, too?"

She didn't want to fight, but Ryan seemed determined, so she wasn't going to just sit there and let him insult her.

Derek looked at her strangely for a moment before turning to his cousin.

"For the sake of our relationship, please back down," Derek asked, praying his cousin would do just that. He didn't want to lose him. He couldn't. But he also couldn't allow him to speak to his fiancée like this. It wasn't right.

"Fine, for you, I will drop it. When's the wedding?"

Jasmine looked at Derek because they'd never discussed a date and she didn't know. Besides, at this point, she really didn't want to talk to Ryan.

"I wanted to get settled into the house first, so I think in about a month. That would give you enough time — right, Jasmine?" Derek asked.

"That's plenty of time," she answered, happy with the subject change, but not really in the mood to discuss a wedding she didn't want to have.

"Well, then. It's settled. We'll get married four weeks from today. Saturday is always a good day to get married, right?" Derek asked.

"That would be fine, but honestly, it doesn't need to be

anything fancy. We can just go to the justice of the peace or something. Jacob could still wear a tuxedo there." She didn't need to keep adding memories that would hurt all the more when it was all over.

"You can't get married like that," Drew piped up as he returned with Jacob. "This is your wedding. You'll want pictures and cake, and of course your guests all want food."

Jasmine was surprised to hear this coming from Drew. For the known playboy in the family to be talking about a wedding? It didn't seem to fit.

"Don't worry. We're having a real wedding," Derek said. He shot Jasmine a warning glance; he'd been doing a lot of warning this evening.

"I was just trying to make things simpler," she said.

"Well, I hate to break up the party, but we better head out. I'm leaving on a business trip tomorrow," Drew said, obviously feeling it wise to get Ryan out of there before any more talk of the past came up. "Thank you for the amazing meal, Jasmine. I can't wait to get back for some more." He bent down to kiss her goodbye.

"Yes, thank you," Ryan said still a bit stiffly before he turned to Jacob. "It was great to meet you, young man. You look just like your dad did when he was your age." He bent down and hugged Jacob, genuinely fond of him already.

Derek walked them to the door and looked Ryan square in the face. "That can't happen again, Ryan. I know you care about me and my father, but she's going to be my wife. I'm not happy about what happened ten years ago, but I have let it go, and I need you to, as well."

Ryan stared for a minute, before his shoulders slumped the tiniest bit. "I just can't forget how devastated you were, how crushed Uncle Dan was. For you, I'll let it go, though. I just wish we knew why she'd done it. Then maybe this would be easier."

"We may never know," Derek said with a sigh.

"Maybe because she didn't do it," Drew said, the voice of reason. Both men turned to him. "Oh, come on. I've been telling you for years that you should talk to her about it. Jasmine isn't a coldhearted witch. How could she have done something like that? Talk to her, Derek, before this thing destroys the family you just got."

Derek didn't say anything; he just watched his cousins head to their vehicle and climb inside. Who was right? Should he listen to Drew? He didn't know.

Walking back inside, he found Jasmine and Jacob cleaning up, and he joined them, making the task go by quickly. They were all tired and the sooner they finished, the sooner this night could come to an end.

When they were done, Jasmine and Derek took Jacob to his room. They took turns reading him his story, and then they left him to the joys of slumber. Jasmine had been so tired the night before that she'd fallen asleep with her son while she read him a story. She realized she had no idea where she was supposed to sleep tonight.

She stepped out into the hallway and just stood there, looking around.

"Problem?" Derek asked.

"I just don't know which is my bedroom. I've been so busy,

I haven't had time to explore upstairs."

"I thought you knew where the master bedroom was," he said.

She looked at him like a deer caught in the headlights. She wasn't ready to fall back into bed with him, but they'd been getting along, and she didn't want the truce to end. She didn't know what to do.

Derek grabbed her by the arms and kissed her mindlessly, molding their bodies together. He had her breathing heavily within seconds. She could so easily give in to his needs — and her own needs, as well. The last two days had her almost screaming in desire.

Last two days, heck! It had been going on all week.

"Look, Derek, I think I've been misleading you. I don't want to sleep with you right now." She struggled to keep her voice from shaking.

Shutters instantly popped up over Derek's eyes. He let her go just as suddenly as he'd grabbed her and then spoke tightly. "I have never had to force a woman to be with me, and I'm not forcing you now. You take the master bedroom, and I'll take one of the guest rooms — for now. You'll soon beg me to join you." His arrogance surprised even him.

"I wouldn't hold your breath," she snarled and then stormed down the hallway, slamming the door for extra emphasis.

Derek thought about going after her for about a minute, but he realized that would just end up with them in bed again, and nothing solved.

He could hold out a little while longer, but if she didn't come to him soon... He strode to the far end of the hall and walked into the only other room with a bed in it for now. He jumped into the shower and let the cold water do its work on his erection — shrinkage — before climbing into a less than comfortable bed.

He lay there for hours, picturing her in his huge four-poster bed, which made him hard and miserable again. That he knew she was just down the hall, sleeping on his sheets, didn't help in the least. He tossed and turned, nearly groaning in frustration.

They had to come to an understanding before too long, or he wasn't going to make it. His body just couldn't take the pain much longer.

Sometime around dawn, he managed to drift off into a less than restful slumber.

CHAPTER TWENTY-SIX

J ASMINE HAD SLEPT unbelievably well. She felt a tiny bit of guilt that she'd taken Derek's bed, but what a bed it was! It was huge and comfortable, and the sheets and covers were soft and silky. She had lain down thinking she'd be awake for hours, but the next thing she knew, it was morning. She stretched out her arms and realized she had no aches anywhere. She should have bought a bed like this one years ago.

She took a long shower in the master bathroom and was delighted when four different shower heads applied varying amounts of pressure over her body. She stayed in there for almost an hour, and the hot water never ran out. She couldn't wait to try the deep tub with the jets. When she was growing up, her father hadn't considered getting such luxuries just for her, though his own bedroom had an en suite bathroom to die for.

Jasmine came down the stairs to find Jacob and Derek sitting at the table, eating cereal. Jacob was his usual talkative self, burbling about his new room and how he couldn't wait to have his friends over.

Derek looked up at her, and she almost gasped out loud at how rumpled he looked. He had dark circles under his eyes, as if he hadn't slept at all, and his clothing was wrinkled. He must have just pulled them straight out of a box, and he probably wasn't thrilled with her decision to unpack their house themselves. She didn't know what to say to him, considering she'd slept better than she ever had in his lovely bed, while, from the looks of him, he had tossed and turned the entire night.

"Good morning," she finally said — almost singing the words, she felt so good.

Derek just grumbled. She had to fight the laughter. The man was even gorgeous when grumpy, rumpled and snarling.

"We should leave soon. I want to go to the furniture store so we can fill this place up," Derek finally said, sipping coffee that seemed to be helping him gain alertness.

"A furniture store? You mean billionaires go to furniture stores?"

"I don't think I understand your question, Jasmine," Derek said, looking with concern at Jacob.

Jasmine caught his glance, and she understood that the man was afraid their son would get too spoiled by his financial elevation. As if that boat hadn't sailed with the red Porsche and the mansion. They had to be realistic. And she had to tease him.

"You know perfectly well what I mean, Derek. The truly rich always hire buyers so they themselves won't have to worry their handsome little heads with mundane tasks like picking out furniture. And they surely don't go to local retailers. Do you think the chandelier in this house came from a shop in the city? Nope. The former owners got things custom made from the best places all around the globe."

"I happen to like doing things the way I always did them. You forget that you grew up a lot more wealthy than I did. Just because I have become successful doesn't mean I've also become lazy, or wasteful. Really. Do you see a chauffeur here? A large staff to do things I can do myself or hire temporary people to do?"

"I figured you were planning on hiring a full staff," she said with a shrug.

"No. I will hire a yard crew and a few staffers to help around the home, but I take pride in doing those things I can do well. I still remember how to mow a lawn. Besides, I can teach Jacob how to do this stuff. It's good for a boy to get some dirt on his hands."

"I guess you still do remember your roots."

She didn't mean it as a putdown, but his eyes narrowed as he tried to determine whether she was saying anything negative about his upbringing. They may not have had money, but his family had always been close, and he was grateful to have grown up without money.

"Do you have a problem with shopping? From my experience, women jump at the chance to do it."

"I enjoy shopping on occasion. I'm just surprised you do," she said, offering him a smile.

"Well, then, it's settled," he said, the tension evaporating as quickly as it had arisen.

"OK, then, if that's the way you really feel," Jasmine said. "Actually, shopping sounds like fun." She really wasn't all that interested in furniture shopping, though. She'd rather get groceries for baking, or books, of course, but she didn't think it was a good time to mention that to Derek — especially considering his bad mood.

"I'm going to go change. It looks like you're ready, so give me about half an hour, and we'll take off," he said, and he practically stomped out of the kitchen.

When Derek came back down the stairs, the dark circles under his eyes didn't keep him from looking as hunky as ever in what he considered his casual clothes — dark slacks and a white button-down shirt. The sexual tension was back with a vengeance.

Jasmine and Jacob followed him out to the SUV, and soon they were off to town. He pulled the car off the road and parked near a huge upscale furniture store. The building had to be at least three stories high. She got out and started to follow them toward the doors when she spotted a secondhand bookstore a few doors down. It also was huge, and it was calling her name.

"Can I meet you guys in the furniture store?" she asked. Derek raised his eyebrows in question. "There's a bookstore over there I want to check out. I should only be a few minutes," she almost pleaded.

"You don't need to buy used books. I can buy you whatever you want new," he said, thoroughly perplexed.

"Oh, no." Jasmine couldn't suppress a sound of horror and outrage at his cluelessness. "There are treasures in there,

Derek. You can find autographed copies and discontinued books. You can find original covers and ancient literature. It's a total treasure hunt in a used bookstore," she explained. "Some people say that book dust is good for you." He didn't notice her sly smile.

"If you really want to…" he said, still amazed by her excitement.

"Perfect. Go ahead and pick out whatever you want for the house. Just leave the library for last, please. Oh, and please don't get anything that is black, or any brown fabric — and I really don't like leather because it makes you sweaty when you sit on it. Other than that, I don't care how we furnish." She said it all in one breath because she really wanted to get to that store. Derek nodded to her, and she turned and rushed through the bookstore's doors.

Derek watched her as she disappeared and then looked at Jacob with wide eyes and raised eyebrows, indicating that he thought Jacob's mother was a little crazy.

"Mom always gets like that when she finds a bookstore she hasn't been to before. She'll be in there all day. I usually try to find a book to read in one of their comfy chairs, 'cause I know it will take forever. She always feels bad about how long she's taking, though, 'cause she buys me a big ice-cream sundae afterward." Jacob was obviously trying to decide whether it was worth it to follow his mom to get the ice cream.

"I'll take you out for ice cream, and you won't have to sit in the bookstore all day," Derek said, as if reading his thoughts.

"Yea," Jacob said, clearly making his choice and following his dad into the furniture store. "Can I have a new bed? I know my bed is good, but I've had it forever, and I really want to get a bunk bed so my friends have somewhere to sleep."

"You can have all new furniture for your room. You're a big boy, and it's time you got a desk and new dresser and other things that fit you better," Derek said, not yet able to deny his son a single thing. "Let's go get your stuff picked out first." He grabbed Jacob's hand.

Jacob's excitement over his new furnishings, his appreciation of everything he got, made Derek feel humbled. The boy thanked the clerk helping them several times. Obviously, Jasmine hadn't spoiled him in a bad way. So the boy was appreciative of things and always polite to everyone.

Derek was beginning to see clearly that Jasmine wasn't the materialistic person he'd once thought. Her choice in furniture — when she bothered with it at all — was another example of who she was. She didn't want the exquisite leather showpiece furniture. She wanted something comfortable for her and her guests. She just didn't care about what people saw when they walked into the room. She was going to be a breath of fresh air in a world of corporate sharks.

After three hours, when they had picked out and ordered furniture for every room in the house except the library, Derek realized he still hadn't seen any sign of Jasmine. "Have you seen your mom yet?" he asked Jacob.

"I warned you. She's forgotten how much time has gone by, like she always does."

"Let's go find her," Derek said. Wasn't the way she got so lost in her books rather endearing?

Jasmine was at the checkout counter in the bookstore.

There were four overflowing bags at her feet and two more on the counter. He looked from her to the bags and back again. She spotted them as the cashier ran her credit card.

"Oh, I'm sorry it took so long. I lost track of time, but they were having a great sale, and there are just so many books here," she explained quickly and then looked from her bags to Derek and her son with a guilty expression.

"We better start hauling these out to the car," Derek said with a smile.

"I know I spent too much, and I'm sorry, but those empty shelves need to be filled — and they had such a great sale," she repeated, following him with two of her own bags. He was going to have to make another trip.

Derek was really curious about what her idea of too much money was. "How much did this all cost you?" he asked.

Her face turned red, and he was thinking she had spent several thousand dollars, although that was chump change for him.

"Two hundred and twenty-four dollars," she mumbled. "OK, and a little change." He could barely hear her and asked her to repeat herself. When she did, he stopped and stared at her. She was feeling guilty about spending two hundred dollars on books!

He started laughing — quietly at first, and then it just kept building up until he was doubled over, he was laughing so hard. He was trying to stop, but he couldn't, and he was shaking so much that his stomach was hurting. It took him about five minutes to get himself under control enough to speak; by that time, Jasmine was staring daggers at him. Jacob was smiling at the sound of his dad's laughter.

"I don't see what you find so amusing," she snapped.

"I can't believe you're standing there with a guilty expression on your face for spending two hundred dollars on books. Seriously, Jasmine. One of the stools we bought today cost twice that much." He was still chuckling.

"Well, whatever," she huffed, and then headed to the furniture store. She was glad he wasn't trying to make her feel guilty over the purchase, but he didn't need to laugh at her. Her father had always told her she wasted her money on books. He couldn't understand why she'd want to read "all that nonsense," as he'd put it. She loved to sink into her fantasy worlds, and she didn't care what anyone had to say about it. OK, maybe she did, just a little, when Derek made fun of her.

Derek and Jacob quickly caught up with her, and although Derek was no longer openly laughing, she could still see the sparkle in his eyes and knew he was fighting it. She finally smiled, realizing that it was a little silly of her to be so uptight. It was just that her father had made her likes seem foolish for so long that she was self-conscious about it, even though she hadn't lived with the man for nine years. Deciding to let it go, she relaxed and vowed to have a good time finding the furniture for the library.

She had to like the fabric, first of all, and tested the different couches by touch. When she found a material she liked, she'd sit on it and see how comfortable it was. She must have done that with a few dozen couches before she found the one she was searching for. The other library furniture was easier to find, and soon they were done.

She didn't know what strings Derek had been able to pull — money and reputation, no doubt — but everything would be delivered the next day. She couldn't wait to get the library all set up.

By the time they got back home, the three of them were dragging their feet. It had been a busy day, but a very successful one.

"How about I order pizza tonight and we sit out back with a fire?" Derek said after they hauled the books into the library.

"That sounds good to me. I can't possibly stand at the kitchen counter for a couple of hours," Jasmine said, her whole body tired.

"I want pepperoni," Jacob said before dashing off.

Jasmine shook her head. "If I could bottle his energy, I would steal from my own son."

"I'll share some of mine," Derek told her as he came closer. He'd promised he wouldn't put any more moves on her, but he couldn't seem to resist.

"I'll see what we have to drink," Jasmine said, quickly sidestepping him and rushing from the room.

Derek groaned in frustration, but he let her go, reminding himself that he wanted her to come to him. She couldn't possibly hold out for much longer. He saw the hunger on her face.

As they all sat by the fire and ate their pizza, Jasmine's gaze managed to meet his more than once. Considering he wasn't able to take his eyes off her, he wasn't surprised.

After tucking Jacob in bed, the two of them stood outside his door for a few tense moments as Derek prayed she'd invite him to her room.

Please, he begged silently.

"Goodnight, Derek. It was a…um…good day," she said softly as her gaze drifted to his mouth.

"All you have to do is ask, Jasmine," he reminded her quietly as he stepped closer.

She inhaled, her eyes widening for an instant before he watched the shutters come down.

"Goodnight," she repeated more firmly, and then he was just watching the sway of her nice round ass as she walked away from him.

It looked like another cold shower tonight. Derek's thoughts were moody as he went in the opposite direction, wondering when he was ever going to get a decent night's sleep again.

CHAPTER TWENTY-SEVEN

S HE WAS GOING to explode. That was it. It was going to happen. Her body was on permanent lockdown and she was dying of frustration.

Two weeks had passed since she'd moved in with Derek and she was so on fire she wasn't sure what to do anymore.

Was he making it easy? Hell, no!

Walking into the kitchen in the mornings, he'd make sure to brush against her. After story time with Jacob at night, his body would press against hers on the way out.

And the looks.

Oh, the looks!

His eyes emitted a constant smoldering heat that seared straight through to her very soul. She wanted him something fierce, but she had to have some pride in herself, didn't she?

Of course, what good would pride do if she were a puddle at his feet? This had to come to an end eventually. She just didn't see how.

As the weeks passed, the tension between Jasmine and

Derek was so thick, the sharpest of knives couldn't have cut it. He continued to let her have the huge master bedroom on her own, but she found it very lonely.

Would she crumble and beg him to join her?

She was dang close to doing it — just as he'd predicted.

They'd been planning the wedding together, but, for the most part, he was doing everything except show up in her stead for the dress fittings. She was in love with the gown he was having made for her; she didn't know how Derek had managed to get it done, but the designer was making a dress that was almost identical to the picture she had created.

Yes, it was a ten-year-old image, but with a few modern twists, it was perfect. Absolutely divine. Why did he care? Was it all because Jacob had asked him?

Somewhere deep inside, she wanted it to be for her. But she dared not hope it was so.

He had certainly thawed toward her, but did that give her a reason to forgive the way he had broken her heart? No. She had to remember the pain she'd gone through, or she was very likely going to end up going through it again — and this time she had a feeling that it would be ten times worse.

But then something in her mind kept saying they'd only been kids then. Couldn't people change? Maybe. But did that excuse the heartbreak? No. Still, they were going to be together for the next nine years. Wouldn't it be so much better if they got along?

Obviously they had some great chemistry together. But that could pass easily after a week or two. She was just so confused.

True to his word, Derek had taken some time off from work,

going in only about half the time, working in the evenings from his home office after Jacob went to bed. He picked him up from school and attended his sporting events. He'd even managed to come to one of the student-teacher conferences.

She didn't know how long he'd be satisfied doing that, but for now, it was nice to share the responsibilities with someone. It was also that much harder to guard her fragile heart.

When Derek did get stuck at the offices, she found herself as disappointed as Jacob. Still, she fought the feelings, and she tried to make the best of the situation by entertaining Jacob in their enormous new home.

He had his sleepover, and ten boys came and spent the night. They fell in love with the swimming pools and basketball court and couldn't figure out which to attack first. They went from activity to activity until they were exhausted and crashed in sleeping bags in the den after watching scary movies and filling up on junk food.

One night Jasmine found herself all alone at the house. Derek had taken Jacob and his friends to a movie, and then dropped Jacob off at a friend's for another sleepover, and the palatial home was so empty. She worked in her home office for a while, but became bored, so she found herself watching a scary movie while hiding beneath a blanket and eating popcorn.

When the doorbell rang, she almost had a heart attack. There was a security gate, she had to remind herself, so whoever was at the door had access and couldn't be an enemy. Still, she went warily to the door and peeked through the viewer.

Her heart sank when she saw Ryan on the other side.

Taking a deep breath of courage, she prepared herself for the ice storm she was about to endure and opened the door.

"Hi, Ryan. Derek isn't here right now," she said as pleasantly as she could muster. It hurt her that he was so cold to her, though. At one time he'd been her friend, like a brother to her.

"I know. May I come in and speak to you?"

His tone gave nothing away, and she knew she could refuse, but what good would that do her? She needed to try to get along with Derek's cousin if she didn't want the next nine years of her life to be completely miserable.

"Sure. What can I do for you?" she asked as she widened the door so he could step inside.

He said nothing as she shut the door and led him to the den, where he looked at her mess with a slight grin, noting the DVD case and her blanket.

"You never could handle scary movies," he said with a small chuckle, which shocked her. Was he teasing her?

She sat down. "No. I don't know why I put myself through the torture of watching them." Now the ball was in his court.

After a few more awkward moments, Ryan sighed as if he'd made a decision. "Look, when all the stuff came down ten years ago, I watched as my cousin was crushed, and my uncle's dreams were shattered. I didn't like it. I've held a grudge. But the reality is that, though Derek seems like he's not getting a hell of a lot of sleep, he's happy. Jacob means the world to him and you're Jacob's mother, which means you're family now. I'm sorry about the way I was with you a couple of weeks ago. I'm going to let it go and want to start fresh with you. Can we do that?"

Ryan looked at her, and his speech left more questions than answers in Jasmine's mind, but he was holding out an olive branch, and she felt that if she didn't take it, there might not be another chance.

As much as she wanted to ask him how she could be considered the responsible one, Jasmine decided to keep the peace instead.

"I would like to start over. I'm sorry if I hurt you in some way. It wasn't intentional, by any means," she said, her voice shaking almost imperceptibly.

Ryan hesitated before stepping closer and holding out his hand. "It's a start," he said with a small smile as he grasped her fingers.

Jasmine was close to tears. She needed family so much, and she was locked in with Derek's now for the next nine years, at least. At one time they had all loved her. Maybe that could happen again; she hoped so, because she was finding that she still loved them more than she should and certainly more than they deserved after the pain they'd put her though.

The heart didn't choose whom to love, though. It was just something that snuck up on you, and before you knew it, you were lost. The people you gave your heart to had the responsibility to protect that love and cherish it. Derek and his family had failed at doing that.

Maybe in time they would earn back the love that she had so freely given them when she was so young.

CHAPTER TWENTY-EIGHT

O NLY A FEW more days until her wedding.
Loneliness was now Jasmine's constant companion.
Since Derek was back in her life, she had to share Jacob. Yes,
the newness of having a father had worn off, but Derek rode
quads with him, took him out on the boat, and had paintball
wars.

She joined them often, but many of the activities just
weren't as fun for her, and when Drew and Ryan joined in, she
felt like an outsider who was desperately and pitifully begging
to fit in.

Derek was working on another business takeover, so after
getting Jacob to bed, he was either locked up in his office at
home or downtown. It was a bit pathetic of her, but she found
herself seeking him out, just for the company.

She'd been living on her own for years, so why did she need
attention now? Why was his reappearance something that
should change her life? Why did a single smile from him seem
to dictate how her day would go?

She was a fool.

This time when the bell rang to notify her that someone was at the front gate, she was almost excited. How sad that she would be happy to greet a delivery person.

"May I help you?" she asked, still feeling a little silly speaking into a box.

"It's Amy. I have materials for Derek," came the sultry female voice.

This was just too much. How dare Derek have one of his ex-girlfriends come to her home. This was now her house and she didn't think it was too much to ask of him not to have a woman he'd once slept with come by.

"Derek is still at the office. You can meet him there," Jasmine said, not even trying to hide her disdain.

"I know that. I was expressly asked to leave these here. He won't be happy if the documents are not here when he returns." Amy's tone indicated that Jasmine was too naïve or too stupid to understand business matters.

With anger coursing through her, Jasmine made the gate open and just hoped Amy came and went quickly.

Meeting Amy at the front door to speed along the visit, Jasmine narrowed her eyes as the woman approached. She didn't look like an employee, but instead the prelude to every man's X-rated fantasy come to life; her incredibly short skirt, skintight blouse and nose-bleed heels put on quite a show. Amy's red nails and matching red lipstick oozed *threat*, and it didn't help Jasmine's confidence that she was greeting this vision in her sweats, without any makeup, and with her hair thrown back in a messy bun.

"Thank you for bringing these over. I'll give them to Derek as soon as he gets home," Jasmine told her.

"He'll be here anytime," Amy said, implying that she had just been with him, and they weren't yet finished doing their… business.

Jasmine narrowed her eyes to pure slits, but didn't say anything to Amy.

"I'm meeting him here. We do have a lot of business to take care of, so I'm sure you can find something else to do," Amy said with a falsely sympathetic smile.

Jasmine's first instinct was to toss the woman out on her doorstep with her fist, but she was a better person than that. "Fine. You can wait in his office," she said through gritted teeth. If Derek was going to bring his tramps into the house, this wouldn't work. She was going to give him a piece of her mind, and she doubted he'd like what she had to say.

She lay down in the library to wait for him to come home, but sleep finally overtook her. When she awoke, it was three in the morning. She sat up quickly and looked out the window. She was relieved to see that Amy's car was gone, but she was still outraged that he'd asked the woman to her house. There were some boundaries you just didn't cross.

She climbed up the stairs and went to his room. He wasn't in there, so instead of searching the house from top to bottom, she decided to get some sleep and then confront him in the morning.

She quickly undressed to her panties and T-shirt and slid beneath the covers. She felt a movement and was startled to find Derek in her bed. "What are you doing here?" she snapped, and she tried to jump from the bed. She was far too angry with him to sleep in the same bed with him. It was pretty damn presumptuous for him to climb into her bed on the night he'd had his ex to her house.

"I got sick of waiting for you to come to me, and I'm tired of the spare room," he said. "I saw you sleeping in the library and didn't want to wake you, but I wasn't to be deterred from coming in here." Derek snaked his arm out to grab her before she could move away. When he realized she was nearly naked, he groaned, and then she felt his lips connect with hers.

The second he started kissing her, she could feel her body's eager response. She attempted one more time to pull away, but he simply increased the pressure of his mouth while his hands started racing over her curves.

They hadn't been together in almost a month, and she was just as hungry as he was after all the heat that had been zapping back and forth between them all that time. She gave up the fight and wrapped her hands around his head to pull him closer. She was burning up, and she needed him to take that sensation away. She forgot all about her worries and just let her body take over.

Derek kept his mouth locked on hers, and his tongue played a tantalizing game. He was pressed to her side, and she could feel his arousal moving against her hip; the heat pooled in her core. Jasmine was desperate to have him inside her.

He moved his lips down her neck and licked along her pounding pulse, making her body squirm beneath him. His hands were stroking up and down her body, and when he brushed over a hardened nipple, her back arched off the bed, as if pleading for more.

He finally moved his mouth down the mounds of her breasts and kissed all around one major spot she needed him to touch. His tongue ran around the areolae around each throbbing nipple in turn, and she tried to twist in his direction so he'd take the bud into his mouth.

He finally did as her body asked him and sucked a tightened nipple into his mouth, causing a ripple of lightning to shoot all the way to her core. She was ready, so ready.

He massaged her chest with his hands while he sucked and licked her swollen breasts. She continued to wriggle underneath him until he finally moved down her stomach. She couldn't stop her body from shaking with need. He kissed down along the smooth surface of her belly and finally reached her aching center, stripping away her panties in no time flat.

As his tongue swiped in and out to caress her folds, she could feel the pressure building inside her. He sucked her sensitive nub into his mouth, and she jerked with the powerful orgasm that washed through her. She continued to convulse as the waves of pleasure coursed all through her. He nibbled his way slowly back upward, careful not to miss a single pleasure spot.

When he brought his lips back down on hers in a gentle caress, she felt as if she could float away on a cloud. It was magical in its intensity. He continued to kiss her mouth and face, and her body began to heat up again.

She boldly flipped him over on his back to return some of the pleasure she had just received. She ran her tongue down his masculine throat, loving the slightly salty taste of his glistening skin.

She continued down over his hard pecs and gloried in the feel of his muscles quivering beneath her tongue. His body was a masterpiece; the texture of his smooth, hard skin held her in its thrall. She moved lower and lower, first down his stomach and then tracing the slight line of hair below his belly button. His hips jerked as she continued on her inexorable path.

She finally reached his pulsing manhood and held it in her hand, rubbing it with firm but gentle fingers. She circled the head, and then licked his body's natural lubrication. His hips thrust upward off the bed, just as hers had.

Jasmine finally lowered her head over the hard shaft and took him deep within her mouth. He groaned as she moved her mouth up and down while also stroking his arousal with her hand. She enjoyed the taste and feel of his silky smooth skin and continued her motions, now faster, as his moans of pleasure egged her on.

He stiffened and then grabbed her head to pull it away. "This is going to end far too fast if you keep doing that," he growled. He pulled her up his body, and she straddled his hips. They had never made love with her on top before, and she was nervous sitting there, with his eyes roaming all over her. The sense of power that she felt, however, was incredibly erotic.

He guided his throbbing arousal toward her entrance, and then she slowly slid down on top of him. As her body lowered, she felt the pressure again building within, and her instincts took over. She started moving up and down him as her body smoothed the way.

She could feel herself start to quiver again, another orgasm building up inside her. He lifted his hands up to knead her breasts as they swayed with each movement she made. He rolled her nipples between his fingers, pinching them gently before smoothing his hands back over the peaks. She could feel the tug all the way down — deep, deep inside her.

He moved one hand downward and started rubbing her swollen nub in a tight circle, building her internal pressure up even more. She sped up as her body tightened, throwing her head back and bracing her hands on the bed. Both their bodies were shaking as she continued moving up and down, again and again.

She thrust down hard and then started convulsing uncontrollably as the orgasm rocked through her entire body. She could feel the fire shooting down her legs as wave after wave of intense pleasure blazed through her. Drained, she slumped forward across his chest. Both their bodies were covered in a fine glaze of sweat, and she slid against his hard chest, making her sensitive nipples quiver.

He grabbed her hips to steady her and thrust up and down in her body until he tensed and cried out as he shot his release deep within her womb. He drew out the pleasure as long as he could, and then grew still as she lay sprawled atop him.

His hands ran up and down her back, smoothing over her backside, making her vibrate with pleasure from his touch. He stroked her hair as they both enjoyed the aftermath of their lovemaking. He finally turned her head and kissed her tenderly. That simple gesture made her fall more deeply in love with him than she had ever been before.

Jasmine finally shifted off him, breaking the connection

between their bodies. She tried to get up, but he refused to release her. Derek kept stroking her hair, neck and back, turning her whole body to jelly.

Their breathing finally got under control, and they lay there in silence for a long while. She was starting to drift off to sleep when he finally spoke.

"Why did you not only open the gates to Amy, but also allow her into our home?"

His voice didn't seem to be filled with anger — just disbelief that she could have done such a thing. She looked up at him in shock. He didn't seem happy that she'd let the woman in. What was going on?

"She told me she had business papers for you and you had a meeting scheduled. She actually made it sound like the two of you were still lovers, which I was going to talk to you about, but you…distracted me," she said, barely above a whisper.

He stared at her for a few moments, stunned. "I have never slept with that woman. As a matter of fact, she was starting to push the boundaries of her employment, and I fired her over a month ago. I hadn't seen her since. I was quite shocked to find her sitting in my den — half-naked, in fact. I immediately escorted her off the premises." His tone of voice that left no doubt he was telling the truth.

Jasmine could only look at him as relief and joy started to pour into her brain.

"It was very obvious that she came here tonight to make a play for me," Derek continued. "But what was plaguing me was that I couldn't figure out why you would have let her in. I guess I never mentioned she was no longer an employee…

Still, I don't understand why you would think we were lovers."

"That day you and I were having lunch together, she was in the bathroom and told me that not only were you lovers, but that she was expecting you to propose marriage to her at any time," she told him. "I thought you really wanted to be with her but found out you had a son and were doing the right thing by him. I know we aren't getting married out of love, but I don't want either of us taking other lovers if we share the same bed."

She turned away from him because she didn't want him to see the pain in her eyes. She didn't want him to know the truth of how much she really cared. It wasn't unreasonable for her to ask him not to take on mistresses. She had a number of reasons, besides love, for making that request.

"I want to share a bed with you, Derek, but only if we're going to be faithful to each other," she finally gained the courage to say. It was very hard for her to do, since the last time she'd opened up her heart to him, he had walked away without a backward glance.

Derek turned her over onto her back again and covered her body with his. She was surprised when his full arousal was at her core, begging to enter. He gently spread her legs open and slipped inside her heat, still wet from their earlier coupling.

She was instantly lost in passion; all rational thought vanished from her mind.

"I have no desire to be with any other woman when I'm with you. I haven't slept with anyone else since you walked back into my life, and I guarantee you that I won't ever do so. You're mine now," he growled before joining his lips to hers.

Jasmine felt a sense of peace as he continued to stroke her

with his hands and his body. They made love several more times that night; neither of them could get enough of each other.

It was a start, something for her to hold onto.

CHAPTER TWENTY-NINE

DEREK STOOD THERE not knowing what to say as Jasmine looked at him with panic in her eyes. Everything was done — well, almost everything — and yet her nerves were shattered.

Tomorrow was the big day, and because of Derek's plans, it had grown far too large — much bigger than she wanted or needed. Everyone in attendance was there for the groom. Wasn't the wedding supposed to be about the bride?

Sure, it was about the groom, too, but every show, every bridal shop, everything she'd ever heard of talked about making the day about the bride.

She felt as if she weren't even needed — which was ridiculous.

It was her wedding!

"You have all of this planned except for one of the most important moments of the ceremony. Who is going to give me away? My father is out of my life, and I have no one else to fill the role," she said, trying to tamp down the panic. She didn't think she'd make it down that aisle all by herself.

"Come on, Jasmine, do you honestly think I'd have forgotten such an important element of your *dream* wedding? The man who will serve as the father of the bride is coming over in a few minutes."

"But who? Is it someone I know?"

"Oh, yes. You once knew him well."

Derek knew that part of his plans for the wedding were cruel, but he had to remind both her and himself what had happened ten years ago. If the two of them were to go forward together and live with a modicum of comfort until Jacob reached his eighteenth birthday, she had to face what she'd done to his family.

It was past time for this confrontation.

She had treated both him and his father as if they were nothing. And worse, she still acted as if her callous inhumanity were nothing, too, as if she hadn't almost destroyed both of them because of her willful obsession with marrying someone of her financial class.

Daniel wasn't overjoyed, to say the least, when Derek told him of his plans to marry Jasmine, but his father felt the same way as he did about the importance of keeping a family together, of having a father and a mother raise their child together when at all possible.

His dad had been heartbroken to learn that he'd missed out on nine years of the life of his first grandchild, but he planned to make up for lost time now that he knew about Jacob. It was time for them to all come together in one room.

This might not be the best moment, but it was better than

waiting until the actual wedding day. Derek could feel his own nerves beginning to fray around the edges.

Daniel was a good man, and he'd been hurt ten years earlier, but for the sake of his grandson, he was willing to let it go. Still, it was with some reluctance that he was coming to meet with Jasmine today and to escort her down the aisle tomorrow.

Derek just wanted to see remorse, to know she was sorry for what she'd done. Maybe, just maybe, they could be happy together while raising Jacob if she would just own up to what she'd done, beg for forgiveness.

He didn't think that was asking too much. He believed she was sorry; he even believed that she cared about him as much as she was capable of caring about anyone. He knew she loved their son. Her entire demeanor changed around Jacob. He truly was the light of her life, and for that Derek cared about her — more than he wanted to.

When Daniel stepped into the room where they were, Derek looked up, waiting for the tension to mount. He was glad that Drew and Ryan had come with his dad. He just didn't know what was going to happen next.

Jasmine looked up and her eyes met Daniel's. Her reaction wasn't what Derek expected. Not by a long shot.

"Daniel?" she gasped as he stepped a bit closer.

"Yes, Jasmine." He was standing a bit stiffly between Ryan and Drew as he tried to decide what he should say next.

"Oh, my gosh," she cried out. Her eyes filled with tears as she ran to him, and she threw her arms around his neck, crying against his chest. "I have missed you so much."

Daniel patted her absently on the back. His eyes connected

with Derek's with an expression of complete shock. Jasmine wasn't behaving at all as any of them had expected — well, anyone except for Drew, who looked at them as if to say, *See, I was right!*

Derek closed his mouth and cleared his throat, trying to get Jasmine's attention. He wasn't sure how his father was feeling about the way Jasmine was clinging to him.

"I'm sorry," she said with a small giggle as she pulled back and wiped her cheek. "Derek said that you are working for Titan Industries. I bet you love that so much, getting to work with your son. He told me you were away on business for the company, but I'm so glad you made it back in time for the wedding. I have told Jacob so much about you that he feels as if he knows you already. He even eats his peanut butter sandwiches just like you do — with butter on them. I don't know when he picked up the habit, and I know it's probably bad for him, but it reminded me of you so much, I didn't have the heart to discourage him. How are you? I'm sorry. I know I'm blabbing and not giving you any time at all to answer. I'll try and shut up."

Taking a deep breath, Jasmine closed her mouth, but she didn't remove her hand from Daniel's arm as she walked with him deeper into the room and joined him on the couch.

She didn't notice the stunned expressions on Ryan and Derek's faces. She didn't see anything except for Daniel, who was now sitting right next to her while Jasmine eagerly awaited his reply.

"Yes, I do work for Titan Industries now. I quite enjoy it, actually," he said after clearing his throat as if he had something caught in it. "My son tells me that you need someone to walk you down the aisle," he murmured.

Jasmine's eyes grew suspiciously bright again. Her voice was low as she answered. "Yes. My…uh…my dad isn't speaking to me."

"I'm sorry to hear that, Jasmine," he said, naturally reaching over and patting her knee.

"It's not as if we were ever really close. There were times when I thought… Never mind. That's the past and it doesn't matter." She looked past him as her mind wandered for just a moment.

"Well, if you don't mind, I would like to escort you," he told her.

"That would be wonderful," she told him, a huge smile breaking across her face. "Thank you, Daniel. Thank you so much."

She leaned forward to hug him again. This time he didn't hesitate long at all before pulling her close.

"I'm going to get Jacob. It's long past time that he met his grandfather," she exclaimed, and jumped up.

Jacob was at a friend's house, so she rushed to the garage for her car. All four men were left standing in the den, looking at each other.

"Now that didn't look like a guilty woman to me," Drew said after they heard Jasmine's car pull from the driveway.

"I just don't understand…" Derek's sentence trailed off as he gazed out the window. None of this made sense anymore.

The sick feeling in his gut was telling him he'd screwed up, and not just a little bit, but so badly that he'd cost himself ten years with the woman he had loved and the boy he now couldn't live without.

"Derek, tell me you actually spoke to Jasmine after speaking with David," Daniel said. Guilt was evident in his expression.

"We'd spoken a couple days earlier. She told me she had a surprise planned for me at the church. She told me to wait there…"

"Did she ever say what it was?" Ryan asked, his own voice quavering and uncertain.

There was a long pause. "No," Derek admitted.

"Are you telling me that all this time, you've been going on nothing but David's word?" Daniel sounded incredulous.

"No! Of course not. Jasmine said…" But what had she really said? Was he a fool?

"You need to talk to her," Drew said. He didn't back down even at Derek's furious scowl.

"Look, it doesn't matter!" Derek insisted. "If we go down this road, I'm afraid we will never come back from it," he admitted.

Ryan spoke again, now firmly. "You also can't move forward if you both don't understand. It kills me to say this, because I was so harsh on her, but I think we may be wrong. Just consider the confusion on her face whenever the past is brought up. What we've believed all these years just doesn't fit with who she was back then, and who she is today. Besides ten years passing, she still seems the same — that young girl full of life and dreams."

"I thought she was innocent all along," Drew muttered, but he made sure it was loud enough for them to all hear.

"Well, good for you." Derek was starting to feel like a fool. He probably was one.

Jasmine returned and her joy wasn't diminished in the least as her son and his grandfather met in delight and wonder. Derek didn't get a chance to speak with her in private before his cousins pulled him from the house. He'd been the one who wanted to keep the tradition of them being apart the night before the wedding. Now he had to regret it.

As she waved goodbye from the doorway, Derek's mind flashed back in time, to the day his life had forever changed;

H E'D FALLEN HEAD over heels for the girl. He'd never thought he was worthy of such a young woman, but he was determined to make himself so. When he ended up helping her with her schoolwork and found a connection with her, he was unable to stay away.

He thought she was so different from the other kids whose parents had money. Her family was the richest in town, and her father reveled in that fact. He walked around in his custom-tailored suits and drove his expensive cars. Hell, the man's house was a showplace, designed to make all the peons worship at his doorstep.

When Derek and Jasmine made love for the first time and he'd realized she'd given him her most sacred gift, he had fallen even more in love. After a few months, he'd proposed marriage, knowing he couldn't live without her.

He planned to head to the city and make something of

himself so he could give her all the things she was used to. He wanted to make sure she never went without anything, even the luxuries her father had surrounded her — or at least himself — with back then. Derek would do, or give her, anything she wanted.

He'd shown up at the church with naïve teenage dreams, a beat-up pickup truck, and a few changes of clothes. When he heard approaching steps, he'd turned in anticipation.

Her father.

The man approached with a sympathetic smile plastered on his face. "Derek, I'm sorry, but Jasmine asked me to come and speak with you," David had said.

Derek didn't understand what was going on, why David would be there instead of Jasmine.

"Jasmine said she couldn't face you," David continued, "but she didn't want to leave here with you. She had second thoughts, I'm afraid. I have some cash here to help you on your way. She said you planned to go to the city, and I want to help you get there." Her father spoke with that same smile on his face. "You know teenage girls. They're in love one minute, and then hate you the next. Oh, I'm sorry, I shouldn't have said that. It's just that Jasmine can be…well, she can be a little spoiled at times, and she just…uh…well, she just decided not to go. Let's just leave it at that." He finished speaking as if he were uncomfortable telling Derek any of this.

Derek felt as if up were now down, as if the world as he'd known it had a completely new face.

Jasmine's father pulled out an envelope stuffed with hundred-dollar bills and held it out toward Derek. Jasmine's father was trying to pay him off. It was as if he were saying, *Thanks for entertaining my daughter, but your services are no longer needed.*

"I don't want your money," Derek spat at him.

David continued holding the envelope out, no doubt amazed that the kid from the wrong side of town wasn't jumping at such a fat wad of cash.

"Jasmine was hoping this would appease your feelings and help you get on with your life," David had the gall to say. She was trying to ensure that her bad-boy mistake now went away. How had she sat in his kitchen, laughed with his father and cousins, while being so cold on the inside? She'd told him she had a surprise for him. Well, she'd succeeded in surprising him, all right. He was stunned and pissed.

"Tell Jasmine *no thank you*," Derek growled and then turned and walked away. He never looked back at David, and he never planned on speaking to Jasmine again. He'd been pissed off enough when David had offered to pay him off, but when he found out it was Jasmine's idea, fury and disgust filled his soul.

By the time he got home, he had cooled down, wondering whether David was making it all up. He'd at least speak to Jasmine — make sure this was really her and not her father.

When he walked in the door, he found his father slumped over at the table, a defeated look on his face. That's when he found out that the loan had been revoked. When Derek asked him to explain, it had been clear. The bank president said Miss Freeman and Mr. Freeman felt it was a bad investment and had threatened to pull their funding from the branch if the loan went forward. The bank was left with no choice.

Derek had just gone dead inside. There was his proof. Yes, she'd told him she had a surprise for him — he'd just never expected it to be one that would destroy his entire family. She wasn't just through with him; she wanted to make it so his entire family would leave what she considered her town.

Well, she'd succeeded.

How wrong he'd been about her. He'd prided himself on his intelligence, and it sickened him. More sickening still was the grief coursing through him when he realized he wouldn't see her again. How weak could a man get?

Right then, he'd vowed that he *would* see her again. As his family pulled away from that small town, he vowed that someday he'd have her begging him to take her back, and then he'd be the one to walk away.

It had taken him only a couple of years to make his first million. He'd met a man the first month he'd been in Seattle, had begun working for him. Those days had been hard, but Derek, Drew and Ryan all worked harder than ever before. They each had something to prove, and within a year, they had more than proved themselves — proved their drive and work ethic.

The old man Derek had met was a multimillionaire who had disinherited his entire family. He'd made each of the cousins an offer they couldn't refuse. He gave them a million dollars to invest. If they lost it, they'd work construction their entire lives. If they profited, then they could keep on investing.

All three boys had invested wisely. When their friend died several years later, they'd been the only ones at his funeral to say goodbye. His money had gone into the charity the four of them had created to help others like them who just needed a break to make something of themselves.

The charity had helped many people since then. Derek still visited his benefactor's grave.

"Hey, are you going to stare out the window all night, or are you going to drink?" Drew asked.

Derek snapped back to the present. Had he been wrong? There'd been proof of what she'd done. He couldn't have been.

He downed his scotch and then picked up his bottle of beer.

"I feel like I'm in the middle of storm," he had to admit.

Ryan was clearly still upset. "Yeah, me too."

The men decided not to speak of the past for the rest of the night. But that didn't really help. They smiled, drank and ate, though none of them had their heart in it.

Tomorrow Derek would get some answers. Tomorrow would be the day he'd find out exactly what had happened that day when Jasmine was supposed to meet him at their little white church.

CHAPTER THIRTY

WEDDING JITTERS? HARDLY.
It didn't count as jitters, surely, if you were having difficulty breathing, your stomach was churning, your heart was palpitating, and you were shivering uncontrollably. Every tick of that damned clock was driving Jasmine half insane.

No, no. She was fine, really.

She'd been plucked, waxed, ironed and forced to submit to every other unimaginable torture, so much so that she didn't recognize the person who stared back at her in the mirror.

She turned around in a slow circle to see herself. The dress was everything she could have ever imagined and so much more. The top was fitted, but from the waist layer upon layer of silk and lace cascaded down. Talk about princesses. Derek had even purchased her a tiara that, she very much suspected, contained real diamonds. She hadn't let it out of her sight for a moment.

The crew he'd hired had done a spectacular job — even she had to admit that she looked beautiful.

She stood in the waiting area of a giant tent with partitions in it, and was crossing her arms across her chest and almost rocking herself, torn between dread and impatience. Derek had been very secretive about where the actual wedding would take place. She was going to be picked up at any moment to be taken to the site. Most brides reveled in the planning of their weddings; Jasmine hadn't minded a bit that Derek had taken over all the planning — the less involvement, she reasoned, the less chance her heart would be shattered.

"Ms. Freeman, your carriage is here," said one of the people standing nearby. She stepped outside and felt tears fill her eyes as she saw the horse-drawn carriage. It was something right out of *Cinderella*. Four white horses were pulling it, and a doorman wearing an old-fashioned tuxedo held the door open for her. Maybe this wedding wouldn't be a disaster. Maybe it *was* out of a fairy tale, and she would live happily ever after. Yes, she really *was* fine.

She glided to the carriage on the soft carpet laid out to the door. One of the attendants was holding up the train of her dress so it wouldn't drag on the ground. The doorman helped her inside, and a couple of people straightened out her dress once she sat down.

Soon the carriage started forward, and she looked out the open windows, wondering what could possibly come next. She hadn't seen Jacob all day and couldn't wait to see what he looked like in his little tuxedo.

Finally, after a long ride, they turned a corner, and then she saw where they were going. Her breath hitched in her chest. Why would he do this? She knew he was angry with her for keeping his son from him, but why would he go to so much trouble to give her the fairy-tale wedding she'd always wanted and then choose the one spot that spelled complete heartbreak for her?

As they pulled up in front of the little church where she'd waited for him, alone and abandoned, ten long years ago, she saw that he'd been busy. The little building, which had once been condemned, was now completely rebuilt and remodeled. It was the same church and looked the way it must have when it was originally built, pure and gleaming and new, and with flowers decorating the steps that led up to the entrance.

She refused to leave the carriage. The doorman stood there, looking slightly panicked. She felt a tear slip down her face and didn't care that she'd most likely ruined her professional makeup job. She didn't care about any of it. Only one thing made a difference to her, and it wasn't a happy one: even on her wedding day, Derek felt he must punish her. Fine. It was done.

She told the carriage driver to take her away, and he looked at her as if she'd lost her mind. She knew he'd been hired by Derek, and her chance of escape that way was probably nonexistent, but she had to try.

While Jasmine was trying to reason with the driver, the church doors opened, and she saw Daniel descending the stairs.

He came up to the carriage and saw the tears flowing down her face. After standing in silence for a few moments, he handed her a linen handkerchief.

"What's the matter, Jasmine?" he asked.

"Why does he want to hurt me so much? I don't understand why he'd pick this place for our wedding. This is the place where he left me standing, waiting for us to begin our life together. Is he even in there, or has this all been one big joke to him?" she blurted out. "I'm sorry, Daniel. I know he's your son, but this is going too far."

Daniel's eyes widened as she spoke, but he said only that he'd be back and turned quickly away from her. He spoke softly to the driver, turned back and patted Jasmine's hand, and then walked into the church. The carriage was suddenly moving once again, and Jasmine was surprised but very happy as they pulled around a corner. He didn't move far, but at least she wasn't in view of the one place that held so many profoundly painful memories.

She was trying to decide whether she should walk away — it would be difficult and she'd make quite a sight in her elaborate dress — or just sit there until the driver decided they could leave. Then the door to the carriage opened again, and Derek slid in beside her. He looked at her face in confusion as her tears silently fell.

"My father said I needed to talk to you, so here I am. We have a deal, Jasmine, and I hope you're smart enough to remember that. I've done everything possible to make this the wedding you wanted."

"Why would you choose this place?" she questioned, as fresh tears escaped.

He stared at her another moment before he spoke. "I thought this place was very fitting. After all, it's the spot where you sent your father to gloat over your betrayal of me and my father. I thought it was ironic."

It was now Jasmine's turn to stare open-mouthed at him. What in heaven's name was he talking about? He was the one who had betrayed her. Her tears dried up in her confusion, and she barely noticed when he grabbed the napkin and cleaned her face up.

"You left me," she barely whispered to him. "Why would you say I betrayed your father? Why are you saying any of this? I don't understand." Being in this spot was making the pain new and fresh. The excruciating memories from that day still haunted her, especially when she looked into her son's face.

They both looked into each other's eyes, surprised and wary.

"Why don't you tell me about that day?" Derek finally asked. He had a sickening feeling deep in his gut.

"Why would you want me to humiliate myself even now?" she replied. She couldn't believe he'd get enjoyment from her pain. And he wasn't going to admit to anything she said. She'd tried to reason with him, tried to resolve her anger with openness, but he always claimed she was lying and walked away.

"Please, just tell me everything that happened after we said goodbye that night," he said, and the change in his tone alerted her that something was wrong. He didn't sound condemning or accusatory, just honestly curious.

So she began to relive the worst day of her life.

She got through most of the story and then came to the part about the loan. "Dad even went to the bank and told them to use my trust fund to back the loan because I'd asked him to. I didn't understand why your dad decided not to open his store, but I figured he just wanted to start over somewhere else." With no more tears left, she waited for him to gloat openly.

Reliving that day was something she'd never hoped to do again, but he'd forced her to do so by bringing her to this place, this spot where her hopes and dreams had both begun and ended.

Derek said nothing as she told him what had happened that morning. He had no doubt that what she said was true. He now understood it had been her father all along, and the man had succeeded in breaking them up.

Her father must have known the child she carried was Derek's, and yet he still hadn't tried to fix things. Though Derek wasn't proud that he'd been driven by such a base motive as revenge for so long, he couldn't help but think that her father had met with what he deserved.

Derek finally took Jasmine's chin in his hands and lifted her sad eyes up to meet his. She looked so heartbroken, and it killed him to know he was responsible for her pain. She hadn't left him, he realized, and his heart was bursting with joy as he captured that thought and repeated it over and over in his brain. He loved her even more now than he had when they were still young and naïve.

How could he have so badly hurt the one person who had loved him so much? He'd been young, but that was no excuse. He should have spoken to her — should have tried to make it right.

He loved the woman she was — both now and then — and he couldn't believe they'd wasted so much time. He kicked himself for purposely trying to hurt her. He felt at an all-time low and vowed to make it up to her for the rest of their lives together.

In silence, he gazed down into her beautiful, sad eyes, and slowly lowered his head to capture her lips. The kiss was gentle and filled with the love that was overflowing from him. He kissed her for several minutes — it was so hard to pull away — before trailing his lips across her cheeks, to kiss away the tears. Then he lowered his head to gently nip the smooth silk of her throat.

She was no longer crying as he continued to drop tender kisses all over her mouth, face and neck. He didn't draw her close against him — he knew how much she loved her gown — but he used his gentle touch to show her the full extent of his love.

He reluctantly withdrew from her and once again looked into her eyes. "Jasmine, I have so much to apologize for — so very much," he started. "I was there at the church that morning. I was there early because I couldn't wait to run away with you."

Her eyes rounded in confusion.

"Your father showed up, Jasmine. He told me you didn't want to be with me any longer, and he offered me a lot of money to start my new life. I actually believed the man. I was so angry with him and extremely angry with you. I thought you'd flung me aside like a piece of trash. To make matters worse, he didn't tell the bank to back the loan. He told the officers there that he'd pull his money from the bank if they did back it. He even got them to tell my father you had went along with it. Your father had a lot of pull in our town, and he used it to hurt my family. Sadly, I vowed to have my revenge from that point on," he said with regret in his voice.

She tried to speak, but he waved her to silence. He had to explain everything.

"I was in so much pain, and that thought of revenge was what motivated me, but when I saw you again, I realized I still loved you. I lied even to myself and said I just wanted to take you to bed and then leave you, like you'd used and left me, but that wasn't the truth. That first time we were together again, after so many years, knocked me off my feet. Every time I touch you, it's never enough. It's so much more than sex. It's because I love you even more today than I did ten years ago. Please tell me you'll forgive me, and that this wedding can be the start of a real marriage."

Jasmine listened to him, hope starting to fill her heart. By the time he was finished speaking, her chest was so full, she didn't understand how her heart wasn't beating right through it. She was saddened to think of all the years they'd wasted, but she realized that none of that mattered anymore, because he loved her and she loved him, and they could be a real family now. They could begin to move forward.

"I'm so sorry, Derek. I really thought you had just walked away from me all those years ago. I never once suspected my father of being involved, but I should have. Over the last few months, I've come to understand so much more about his character, about his flaws. I'm sorry he cost your father that business and cost you so many years of Jacob's childhood. I should have tried harder to find you."

He brought his lips back down to hers and kissed her with

so much hunger and love that she was tempted to skip out on the wedding and tell the driver to take them back home. As if he could read her thoughts, he quickly pulled back and leapt out of the carriage.

"You're far too tempting, woman. We have a wedding to get to," he said with a brilliant smile. He spoke to the driver and then jogged back to the church, singing "Get Me to the Church on Time." This time, when the carriage pulled up in front, she was more than ready to step from its doors. She didn't even care about her ruined makeup, or her slightly mussed hair. She just wanted to reach Derek and not lose one more minute of their time together.

The driver clearly wasn't taking any chances of a runaway bride again — as soon as she was clear of the carriage, he drove away. She giggled a bit at the speed with which he left.

She stood on the wide carpet and could feel her nerves catching hold of her. But before her heart could thunder too loudly, the front doors opened just as the attendants got her dress situated. Daniel was once again walking down the steps and coming toward her.

"Oh, Daniel. I can't believe you offered to walk me down the aisle when you believed I'd done something so horrible to you. What a truly great man you are."

Seeing the genuine gratitude in her eyes, he leaned down and kissed her on the cheek. She was filled with warmth from the easy acceptance of this wonderful man.

"Ah, Jasmine. I am nothing but a silly old fool," Derek's father said. "I knew you back then, knew what a heart of gold you had, and yet I took the word of virtual strangers. I just pray that you will forgive me."

Jasmine was filled with love for this amazing man. He was standing in to be the kind of dad her own should have been. Tears once again welled up in her eyes, causing the attendants around her to groan.

"There's nothing to forgive," she whispered to Daniel.

"Now don't start crying again, young lady, or we'll never get you to that altar," Daniel said with a gentle laugh.

Jasmine gazed up into his eyes, and she noticed that they were suspiciously bright, too.

"Then you'd better get me down that aisle quickly, because I can't promise not to cry at this point."

Their arms intertwined and, slowly, they made their way to the front of the church. The double doors were opened, and Jasmine was left speechless by what she saw inside. There were thousands of twinkling lights strung throughout the church, and the scent of roses wafted in the air from the hundreds of floral arrangements adorning the interior from the narthex and nave to the altar.

The small church was packed from front to back with guests who all stood and turned toward her. She had to fight to keep the tears from falling once again. She looked down the aisle, strewn with rose petals, to Derek, who made her breath catch in her throat as she saw him at the front with Jacob by his side. Drew and Ryan were standing in the spot where bridesmaids would normally be, so her side didn't look empty.

The men were a stunning sight, all dressed in classic tuxedos with tails and white ties. Jacob was grinning at her as she made her way slowly down the aisle; it seemed to be taking everything in him not to run up and hug her. She felt the same way.

When her eyes connected once again with Derek's, the rest of the world seemed to fade away, and she could look nowhere else. The man was beautiful, and she couldn't believe he was hers, all hers She picked up her pace, without even realizing what she was doing, until she heard a chuckle from Daniel.

They reached the pulpit, and then Daniel reached down and kissed her gently on the cheek before taking his place next to her son. The princess in her fluffy white dress stood secure in the middle of a sea of masculinity, and she repeated the vows that meant forever while gazing into Derek's eyes.

At the beginning of their first dance, when Derek drew her lovingly into his arms, her heart burst in pure happiness. He looked at her as if she were a hidden treasure he'd just discovered, and the lump in her throat wouldn't go away.

"Thank you for taking such great care of my son," he said as he spun her around. "I'm sorry you had to do it alone all those years. I'm sorry you thought I had walked away from you. I'm a real fool to think anything could have made you do that. You're the purest person I've ever known, and I promise you I'll spend the rest of my life proving how special you are to me."

"I missed you every day," Jasmine told him. "When I looked at our son, I was filled with a mixture of joy and sadness. The older he got, the more I missed you. Still, the earlier days were the hardest because I wanted to share all those moments with you. I've never felt such pain as when I thought I'd never be in your arms again. I was never really able to hate you, though I tried."

"We won't even talk again about the bad times and the misunderstandings and your father's lies. From this day forward, we'll focus only on our future. If you can forgive an utter fool, I promise to love you the rest of our lives."

She wrapped her arms more tightly around his neck. She'd never have to withhold her feelings from him again.

Drew stood up, and the room fell silent, except for the noise of clinking glasses. "It's time for the toasts," Drew said. "Derek and I are closer than even siblings could ever possibly be. He and Ryan are about the only two beings on this planet I would've taken a bullet for — until today. I've known Jasmine for many years, and only one thing ever outshone her beauty — her truly kind heart. It's such a great privilege to have her as a part of my family. I'm so glad to have her and Jacob as additions, and that makes two more people I'd take a bullet for," he said. "To a lifetime of happiness and many more babies to come. Congratulations, Derek and Jasmine."

The crowd thundered its applause.

Jasmine managed to break away from Derek to throw her arms around Drew and thank him for his kind words. She then embraced Ryan and told him how much she loved him as well. The night continued on with laughter, dancing and a whole lot of kissing, and Jasmine couldn't help feeling a little sad when it all ended.

Daniel had insisted on keeping Jacob for a few days so the newlyweds could have a proper honeymoon, and she knew Jacob's grandfather would spoil him rotten. The boy had at first been apprehensive about having his mom gone, but he got along so well with his grandpa that it all worked out fine.

As Derek and Jasmine ran through the birdseed out to the awaiting carriage, she believed her life couldn't be any better than it was at that moment.

She was wrong. When Derek took her to his bed as his wife, she learned that passion and love together made everything grow stronger and better with each new day.

EPILOGUE

"MMM, I SEE you are in your favorite spot of the house again," Derek whispered in her ear as he wrapped his arms around the middle of his wife's rapidly expanding stomach.

"My second-favorite room," she corrected as she turned around and kissed Derek. "Or my third; I'm torn between this room and the library, and, of course, our bedroom."

"You do realize that the caterers can finish this meal without your input, right?" he said with a laugh.

"Are you saying they cook better than I do?" she asked, narrowing her eyes teasingly.

"I would never be such a fool as to say that." He leaned forward and kissed her nose.

Since they'd spent their honeymoon at home, Derek planned to take her somewhere extra-special for their anniversary. As a matter of fact, he'd vowed to take her and Jacob to every one of Drew's magical resorts, and they were going off on their first adventure to one of them soon.

On the first night of their married lives, he'd taken the prenuptial agreement and burnt it in the fireplace as a sign of good faith. The next week, he'd called his attorney and had the document destroyed for good. His trust in her was overwhelming, and she knew nothing would ever keep them apart again — especially the lies of a bitter old man.

"You know you've made my happily-ever-after come true, right?" she said, cuddling against his chest as close as her pregnant belly would allow.

"I owe you a lifetime worth of happily-ever-afters. You bring so much joy, Jasmine. I was half a man before you, and now I feel complete." He leaned down and took her lips in a slow, hungry kiss.

"As much as I'd love to take this upstairs, your family will be here at any minute for our son's tenth birthday party," she reminded him.

Derek let her go with some reluctance, and she turned too quickly, bumping her protruding stomach into the island. The baby kicked inside her as if to say, "Hey! Watch it, Mom!" She laughed out loud as she rubbed the spot where she'd felt the child move.

"Be careful, darling. You have very precious cargo in there." Derek wrapped her in his arms again.

"Oh, Derek, it's nothing. However, your son or daughter didn't like it; the child decided to kick back, and good," she said with another giggle.

Derek immediately dropped to his knees and lifted her shirt over her stomach to check the entire area, then he leaned forward and gently kissed her bump.

"Are you OK? Maybe we should go into the hospital just to make sure." Worry was written clearly between his eyebrows as he rose to his feet. Before she could say anything, he picked her up and started to head toward the garage.

"Derek, put me down right this minute. I'm fine. It was just a little bump. I need to get used to this big belly." She secretly enjoyed his overprotectiveness.

Though he didn't seem happy about it, he gently lowered her to the ground, "I'm just saying, it's better safe than sorry," he mumbled, and she could tell he was still thinking about making her see a doctor.

She laughed more and pulled him in close for another kiss. She had learned quickly how to distract him, and her kisses would surely silence him. Soon, they were both groaning with passion; he rubbed his hands down her body and gripped her behind. Jasmine forgot all about the party.

"OK, you two are disgustingly happy together," Drew said as he walked into the room. "And it makes the rest of us sick, so can you please — for two minutes — manage to tear yourselves apart?"

Derek groaned in frustration, then nearly pouted when Jasmine let him go. Drew received only a scowl from him, but Jasmine walked over to Derek's cousin and pulled his head down close so she could kiss his cheek.

"You know you're all talk. You're going to fall head over heels in love soon, and then I'll get to pick on you. I love you to pieces, Drew Titan, and the lucky woman who gets to spend her life with you will be incredibly special."

Drew's face turned red as he pulled Jasmine into a gentle

hug.

"OK, Drew, find your own woman, and leave mine alone," Derek told his cousin before dragging him from the room.

Jasmine watched them leave, her heart swollen with love. She had finally spoken to her father, and it hadn't gone well. He was an unhappy man who was running away from his problems. It grieved her that he'd rather she wasn't in his life, but she had a new family, and they were people you were proud to call your own.

It was probably better this way, since David would most likely be spending time in prison soon. The district attorney had finally amassed enough evidence to prosecute and the trial was starting next month. Jasmine found that she really didn't want to be there, so she was going to stay out of it unless she was forced to testify.

"Something smells good in here, but make sure you don't overdo it," Ryan said as he walked into the kitchen just as Jasmine stepped back through the doors. Yes, she was driving the caterers crazy, but it wasn't every day her son turned ten.

"You boys worry far too much, you know," Jasmine told him. "This may surprise you, but women are having babies every single day and they are just fine." She gave him a hug. "The others are at the pool, so go on out and play."

"Why don't you take a break and join us so we at least have a great view?" he asked with a waggle of his eyebrows. It was so nice that everything was back to normal with Ryan. He was much quieter than Drew, but he had a truly beautiful heart.

"I think I'll do that. My feet can use a break." She threaded her arm through his and walked out back.

"What's up with you lousy jerks pawing my wife?" Derek said as they stepped out the door.

"Look, your wife is so extremely hot, it's impossible for us to keep our hands off her," Ryan said, as he bent to kiss her cheek. She smacked him lightly before she settled down into one of the comfortable lounge chairs.

Derek immediately headed over and, pulling up a chair, lifted her feet onto his lap. He started rubbing the tender soles, making her moan in pleasure as he used just the right amount of pressure.

"You can stop in about ten years," she said with a purr of satisfaction. He leaned over and kissed her gently before continuing. She couldn't believe how much she loved him, this man she'd lost for too many years. But now, they had forever stretched before them, and the past was just that — the past. They'd moved on and were both happier than she ever imagined she'd be.

The baby kicked her gently in the ribs, and she smiled. "Don't worry. I know you're there," she whispered, and then she counted her blessings, as she knew she'd do the rest of her life.

If you liked Derek's story, the series continues with Drew's story in:

THE TYCOON'S VACATION

Read an excerpt now:

Prologue

Y OU DON'T KNOW what you're missing out on, Drew. I've never been as happy as I am now. I love you and Ryan, you know that, but having a wife and children is unlike anything you can imagine. I feel…fulfilled. The void you didn't even know was there is replaced by pure love." Derek spoke to his cousin as they sat by the pool, having a drink and catching up.

"I think Jasmine is about the most perfect woman in this universe, but marriage is for you – not me. I'm a confirmed bachelor, and I want it to stay that way. Why should I settle down with just one lady, when I can have a new one on my arm anytime I want?" Drew flashed a wicked smile. Though he said the words, he didn't believe them. He'd watched his newlywed cousin, happily married, and he felt a longing for something more. He refused to admit that out loud, though. He had a great life and there was no reason to change anything.

"I used to feel the same way – that was until Jasmine came back into my life. Now I just think of all the wasted years we could've been together," Derek said. Drew winced at the pain in his cousin's voice. Derek had finally married his childhood sweetheart, but circumstances had kept them apart for ten years. Drew knew it pained Derek to think about the years forever lost.

"I think I'm just restless because I need a vacation. I've been working non-stop lately and it's time to pick one of my resorts and go soak up some sun and lay on the beach. I'm sure I can find a few pretty ladies to enjoy the time with," he said.

Drew had always been okay with keeping things simple when it came to women. That had always been enough for him, so he figured the restlessness really was just the fact that he was working too hard. The old saying seemed to be quite fitting, all work and no play...

"What are you boys discussing with such serious expressions on your faces?" Jasmine asked. She walked out, carrying her beautiful baby girl and Drew immediately held out his arms to take her. He'd fallen head over heels in love with his niece, and could even imagine himself with a few of his own children someday. He shook off the thought since he couldn't have the babies without a wife.

"Drew was just talking about chasing tail," Derek said as he grabbed Jasmine around the waist and settled her onto his lap. She giggled, before bending down to kiss him. Drew cleared his throat to remind them he was still there.

"Sorry, Drew," Jasmine mumbled as a pretty blush stole over her features.

"Want to babysit?" Derek asked, though it wasn't really a question. He also wasn't the least bit sorry. Before Drew had a chance to say anything, Derek rose with Jasmine still in his arms and carried her off. Her feeble protests faded as the two disappeared into the house.

Britney's irresistible blue eyes and toothless smile tugged at Drew's heart. He blew raspberries on her stomach, which made her giggle and pat his face.

"I know your parents are a bit nutty, but you have to love them anyway," he said. He didn't feel foolish talking normally to her, even though she had no idea what he was saying. He found himself babysitting for a long time before the happy couple returned.

He raised his brows at his cousin, who just shrugged as if to say he couldn't help himself. Jasmine apologized for her husband's behavior and took Britney back so she could get her ready for bed. His arms felt instantly empty without the baby nestled against him.

"I'm going to take off now since my presence here is obviously not needed," Drew said with a huge smile.

"Hey, you know you're always wanted here," Derek told him. Drew knew he meant the words. He'd been an only child, but it had never seemed that way. Having Derek and Ryan was even better than having siblings. Their bond was unbreakable.

"I know. That's why I keep coming back. I'm going to take everyone's advice, though, and take that vacation. I'm sure once I get away from work, I'll feel better, and can get back to myself."

"Don't stay away too long. You know how quickly Britney is growing up," Derek said as he walked Drew to the door.

"I can't believe how quickly she's growing. It seems like only yesterday she was born, and look at her, already a few months old. I won't be gone long – she'd miss me too much. Plus, I'm thinking it's time to start slowing down. Traveling the world isn't holding the same appeal it used to when I first started building these resorts. Now that you're all settled down, I look forward to coming back. I think it's your wife's cooking. I swear I've put on twenty pounds," he said, while rubbing his flat stomach.

"I understand. I'm going to have to go to the tailor to let all my pants out," Derek agreed, while rubbing his own impressive stomach. They shook hands and Drew walked out. He sat in his car and gazed at his cousin's home with the warm lights inviting a person to step inside. He shook his head as he started his silver Bugatti Veyron, listening to the twelve-hundred horsepower engine roar to life. He grinned as he started down the road. Yeah, he'd get back to his normal self. Kids and luxury vehicles didn't go hand in hand, he silently reminded himself.

He called his pilot as he headed to the airport, knowing his jet would be fueled and ready by the time he got there. Some sun and surf would wash all thoughts of marriage and children away. He simply wasn't the marrying kind, not like Derek was.

Drew arrived at the airport and parked his car before boarding his jet and sitting down. He looked around at what he had and sighed. Life was good. Derek's words of something missing nudged at him from the back of his mind, but he pushed them back.

Once the plane was airborne, he sipped his drink and laid his head back against the seat. The world seemed to slow down as he closed his eyes and took a few deep breaths. *Yeah*, he thought, *this is what I needed*. After a few days of nothing but surf, sun, and sand, everything would return to normal.

Chapter One

TRINITY LAY ON an oversized towel, a sigh of ecstasy escaping her lips. She felt the sun shine down on her closed eyelids. It melted the tension from her tight shoulders. She imagined herself floating away on the crystal clear water that lapped on the beach.

This was the first impulsive thing she'd done in her life. She had always been a responsible person, but after being walked all over by yet another boyfriend, she had packed one bag, hopped on a jet, and ended up on a secluded island off the North Coast of Spain. The last leg of her journey had been on a small charter aircraft with spectacular views of the Mediterranean Sea. She'd been unable to take her eyes away from the window as the aircraft circled the island before landing in this paradise.

She'd spent every dime she'd strictly saved over the last ten years, on the mega expensive, all-inclusive resort. She knew every penny of it was worth eating ramen noodles for the next year.

Her life had been flipped upside down a few days ago, making her snap. She'd always been the people pleaser in her group of friends, and in the few romantic relationships she'd been in. She was stubborn to a fault with herself, always setting high goals to achieve, but when it came to others she was a pushover. She vowed to never let that happen again.

Her last relationship was the reason she was now feeling the warmth of the sun and her bank account was empty. Her mouth stretched out in a pleased grin. As she became too warm, she stood up and headed toward the inviting water. She tried not to think about her ex, but the man invaded her thoughts. Her brows puckered as she frowned at the memory of another relationship gone wrong.

Trinity's thoughts flashed back to a few days before. She'd been with her supposedly straight-laced boyfriend for six months and felt it was time to take the next step. One thing about him that had impressed her so much was his willingness to wait for her to be ready to go to bed.

As she stood in front of her mirror, looking at the dress molded to her body, she took a deep breath for courage. Excitement pulsed through her as she thought about their bodies entwined in a night of lovemaking. She'd never been one to have casual affairs, only having taken that final step with two other men – and those had turned out to be disasters. She was starting to feel like sex would be more of a chore for her, versus a pleasure. She was determined to prove herself wrong with this boyfriend, though. They got along perfectly. So what if he didn't cause her stomach to quiver like she'd read in so many romance books. She was sure when they really started getting into the act, she'd feel the explosion she searched for.

Trinity had the key to his place. He'd been on a business trip the previous month and she had looked after his plants. She'd forgotten she still had it, but was grateful. She had her arms full of every seduction tool she could think of – candles, lotions, oils… even whipped cream. Her face lit with a smile as she turned the door knob.

It was such a cliché, because of course she opened the door, her heart racing with anticipation, only to find the creep in bed with his secretary. He begged Trinity to stay, while the naked woman next to him glared daggers at her. It was almost laughable – it would've been, had she not been so crushed. He promised it was a one-time thing, that he temporarily lost his mind. One thought broke through her disbelief: *pathetic*.

As she'd walked out the door, she vowed she was done with businessmen for good. She was tired of being their perfect girlfriend, doing their laundry, cleaning their places, and being at their beck and call. Powerful men seemed to expect servants instead of wives. Well, she was done being the girl everyone could depend on. She was done always playing it safe. She was certainly done with being a doormat.

Trinity dove into the water and swam until her arms started to ache as her thoughts continued to run through her last couple of days.

She'd gotten into her car and drove back to her boring, beige apartment. As she looked around in disgust, something inside her started to shatter – as if she was truly casting off her old self. That's when she started searching the internet for exotic resorts. She'd found a brand new resort on an island off of the coast of Spain. It had everything she wanted and more so she booked her ticket and then went to the mall to purchase a new bikini.

When she returned home after the stores closed, she was amazed to realize she hadn't cried. Not one tear was shed for the man she'd spent months with. It was at that moment she realized she didn't love him, and she certainly didn't need him. She had a hard time falling asleep, she was so excited over her impulsive trip.

Her first night on the island, a spectacular sunset had triggered the first tears she'd shed for a long time. The sheer beauty of colors splashed across the sky caused more emotion in her than any man ever had. She was exhausted as she climbed back up to her room. Finally, the last couple days caught up to her, and she fell into a deep, healing sleep.

For a few seconds after she woke up that morning, she'd been confused about where she was. She'd sipped a few too many margaritas in the outdoor bar the night before. Once it all came back to her, she couldn't keep the smile from her face. She'd slipped on her incredibly daring bikini, and then headed to the resort's private beach.

Trinity snapped back to the present and realized how far out she'd gone. She was a good swimmer, but she was so far from shore, the resort looked like a hut. She turned around and started heading back in. As her mind emptied of all thought, she focused on only the warmth from the sun and the coolness of the glorious water. There was no stress, no feelings of regret, and no doubt she'd made the right choice. That's all she felt, until something crashed into her head. There was a moment of shooting pain and then blackness. Her last thought, before she sunk beneath the surface of the water, was that her room was non-refundable.

D REW CLIMBED OUT of his jet and let the island's intense heat soak through him. He was ready to change clothes and hit the waves. He climbed into the golf cart waiting for him with a smile. It sure was a change from home.

He swept down the small hill, from the even smaller airport, and grinned as his resort came into view. He loved his job – he loved finding the perfect spot of paradise to build an exquisite work of architecture. He was involved from the beginning – choosing the land, the exact placement on that land, and then being a part of the creation of every nook and cranny of his unique design. Not one of his resorts looked the same, and he was proud of that fact. His loyal customers could go to a different one each year and get a new and unique experience.

He walked in the employee entrance, watching as the staff moved around, performing efficiently in the clean space. It took several moments for someone to notice him.

"Hello, Mr. Titan. I was surprised when I saw your jet land," John, his head of security, said as he approached with his hand out.

"Hi, John. I'm here on vacation. Let everyone know that I'm not the boss the next several days. If there's a problem, deal with it like you normally would if I'm not here," Drew said. He enjoyed the look of surprise on John's face. He had to admit that he was a bit of a workaholic.

"Of course, sir," John replied. He quickly walked away to inform the staff of Drew's request, while Drew went to his suite and changed.

It took him no time to grab his board and start paddling out into the deep water. The waves were too mellow for his taste, and he'd have to go further than usual. He was okay with that, though. Nothing was going to upset his perfect mood.

As he paddled further out to sea, he felt every last ounce of stress drift away into the sea. Suddenly, he hit something and turned his head to try and find what he'd run into. He barely caught a glimpse of a body as it sunk below the water's surface.

"What the hell?" He dove off his board to retrieve the person. No one was ever out this far unless they were surfing. He supposed their board could've gotten away from them, but he didn't see one floating anywhere without a rider.

He caught the person before they sunk too far, realizing it was a woman. He threw her on his board and quickly paddled back to shore, where he immediately began CPR. He was panicked until she choked up some water and started to breathe again. That's when he finally allowed himself to sit back and assess the situation.

She looked up at him through bloodshot eyes and groaned. Her hand immediately reached for her head, where he could already see a large lump forming. Drew's eyes widened as his body tightened at the sight of her. He'd just about killed the girl, and had no business gawking at her as if she were some bikini model on display for his pleasure.

She was spectacular, though, in an understated girl-next-door kind of way. She had long blonde hair that was currently plastered over her face. Her deep emerald eyes were staring at him with confusion, and even though she was becoming visibly worried, there was still a sparkle deep within their depths that was holding him captive to her gaze.

Her body was toned and yet curvy and feminine with hips just the right size for his hands to grip onto. He shook his head, casting the improper thought from his mind. Instead, he focused on her medical needs.

She was far too pale to be so unprotected on these beaches. He could already see a tint of red covering her fair skin. The burn was going to bother her in the morning if she didn't get plenty of lotion on.

His body went into overdrive at the thought of rubbing lotion across her smooth skin. He could almost picture his hands gliding down the slight dent of her waist, rubbing across her gently rising hip, and over the lushness of her butt... Drew groaned before he pulled himself together.

What the hell is wrong with me, he shouted in his head. He'd almost drowned the poor woman, and now he was mentally taking her on a public beach. A stiff drink and a night of unattached sex would fix him, he reasoned – just not the woman he'd damaged.

Still no words had been spoken as he reached down and lifted her into his arms. His only thought should've been on getting her the medical attention she needed, not on bedding her. Several people rushed forward as they tuned in to what had happened.

"Can we help?" Two guys were standing next to Drew,

looking from him to the woman.

"I'll get her inside, thanks," Drew responded before easily carrying her to the resort.

Each step he took, the swell of her breasts bounced against his chest, causing his breathing to quicken as if he were running a marathon. Hopefully, she thought he was just overexerted instead of excited. The scent of her hair was causing more erotic images to pop into his mind.

Her tiny bikini wasn't hiding much from his view and he wanted to move the top those last couple of inches. It was almost a burning need to see if her peaks were soft and pink, or dark and red. He groaned out loud as he tried to think of anything but devouring the stranger in his arms. Damn, he wasn't a horny teenager, but a grown man. He sure as hell wasn't acting like it, though.

"What happened?" She asked in a scratchy voice. He jumped a little at her first words. He was so lost in his own fantasies, he hadn't even bothered to explain anything to her. As he watched her flinch from the pain of speaking, his guilt over hitting her took his mind off of his mental devouring of her.

"I hit you with my surfboard. You went under the water, but only for a few seconds before I got you out. I performed CPR, and I'm sure your throats tender, but we're going to the first aid station to see if there's any damage," he answered as he entered the air conditioned building. She immediately began to shiver and his eyes were once again drawn to her now beaded nipples. He picked up his pace.

He reached the first aid station, laid her down, and quickly found a blanket to cover her. It was both for her benefit, and his. The doctor was there within minutes, as he kept one on call at the resort twenty-four hours a day. Too many things could go wrong, even in paradise, and they were very isolated. He wanted his guests to know that help was always available, night or day.

The woman drifted to sleep before the doctor could begin his examination. Drew looked on in concern. Head trauma victims were supposed to stay awake, weren't they?

"Should we wake her up?"

"Why don't you tell me what happened, then I'll know if she should be awake or not," the doctor answered as he looked at the nasty lump first.

Drew explained what had happened while the doctor examined her thoroughly. After what seemed like forever he finally turned back to Drew.

"She'll be just fine. Her head is going to hurt pretty badly, but other than that, there's no permanent damage. She can't be alone tonight, so if no one is with her, she needs to stay here until morning. With a head injury, she has to be woken every hour to be safe. She doesn't have to get up, but we want to make sure she doesn't slip into a coma. She also needs to rub this aloe lotion on her skin. I'm more concerned about her burn than anything else."

The resort's biggest medical issue was always sunburned clients. They weren't used to the intense heat of the island and never protected themselves enough even though there were warning signs placed everywhere and the resort provided free sunblock in each room.

"I'll make sure she's taken care of," Drew said and shook her awake. She partially opened her eyes, as if even that much took real effort.

"What's your full name?" Drew asked.

"Trinity Mathews," she responded with a smile that lit up her face, causing his breath to quicken. He was trying to shake off the dizzying effect she was having on him, but nothing seemed to be working.

"Are you here with anyone?" As he asked, he found himself holding his breath. He'd noticed she wasn't wearing a ring, but that didn't mean anything.

"No, I'm on my own," she answered, then winced again. "My head really hurts."

"The doctor gave you a shot for that. It should kick in soon," he told her. She lay back down and drifted to sleep once more. Drew sent a staff member to get the information he needed on Trinity. She came back quickly and confirmed Trinity was there alone and staying in one of the smaller rooms in the hotel. That was changing. Ms. Mathews had just earned an upgrade to his nicest suite.

He called a bellhop and had him go up ahead to have him move her things to the executive suite. He then had to wake her back up again.

"Trinity, the resort is moving you to a suite." She smiled as if she was only half listening, then closed her eyes again. Drew picked her back up, leaving the blanket around her before he trudged through the hotel. He didn't need to stare at temptation any longer, and he certainly didn't want other men looking.

He made it to the elevator and rode it to the top floor. There were only a few rooms on that level and a special room key was needed to even get up there. The bellhop held the door open so Drew could get Trinity inside without hitting her head again. He went straight for one of the large beds and laid her down.

She snuggled into the feather mattress and sighed. The doorman left and Drew found himself alone with the gorgeous female he couldn't quit fantasizing about. He shook her awake again and she glared at him. He barely managed to suppress the smile wanting to break out on his face. It was obvious she was getting tired of him waking her up.

"Trinity, I'm sorry to wake you, but the doctor said you need to get this lotion on or your skin will blister," he said. The drug the doctor had given her must have been working because her eyes closed again and she was out cold, completely ignoring his words.

Drew groaned as he realized he was going to have to apply the lotion. He looked skyward and wondered how much he could take of touching her supple body. He sang out loud as he poured the lotion into his hands and began rubbing them together. He didn't want to shock her with cold lotion on top of everything else. Once he rubbed it around his hands, wasting time, he finally began applying it to her legs.

He figured if he started with her legs, it would be easier on his libido. He was wrong, so very wrong. By the time he finished smoothing the cream over her incredibly lush body, he had a throbbing erection and could barely breathe. On top of that, sweat was dripping off his brow.

He walked from the room and quickly jumped into an

icy cold shower. He stayed under the excruciating spray until his skin started turning blue and his goose bumps had their own goose bumps. Once Drew finally could move his muscles again, he decided to grab his laptop and work. He couldn't leave Trinity alone so he had a lot of time to kill.

He woke her every hour. Each time, she'd give him a groggy answer before shutting her eyes again and falling back to sleep. The twenty-four hours couldn't end soon enough, because each time he saw her lying in the huge bed, he wanted nothing more than to climb in with her. He finally fell asleep in the middle of the night, exhaustion taking over from his long flight and tiring day.

A S TRINITY SLOWLY awoke, her only thought was that she was starving. Her stomach rumbled loudly when she smelled a delicious aroma drifting toward her. As she turned over and opened her eyes, she realized she wasn't in her room. Before panic set in, she closed her eyes and concentrated. Had she gotten drunk and gone to a guy's room? That wasn't like her. Slowly, her memory came flooding in. It was a little hazy around the edges, but she remembered getting hit in the head.

One minute she was swimming, and then the next thing she remembered was about the sexiest guy she'd ever seen was leaning over her with panic filled eyes. She couldn't remember much about his face, other than he'd been stunning enough to take her breath away, and that his eyes had been the same striking color as the sea behind him.

She vaguely recalled him carrying her, and that her head had been throbbing. Sleep had been a blessed relief because every time someone woke her up, she had to endure the pain.

Trinity lifted her hand to her head and felt the area. There was a large lump on the side, but her headache was gone. In fact, she felt pretty good, other than a severely empty stomach.

She climbed from the bed and looked in the closet, relieved to find her clothes there. Maybe she'd hit her head harder than she thought, and the hotel had moved her and she just couldn't remember. She slipped on a sundress and followed her nose.

Trinity came to a standstill when she saw the man from the beach sitting at a table, removing lids from food dishes. As she took in his features, more of her memory came flooding back, and she couldn't believe she'd forgotten a single thing about him, not his washboard abs or sexily defined arms – not even after years in a coma would he be forgettable.

Finally, he looked up and she couldn't quit staring. He quickly stood and pulled out a chair for her. She had to blink twice to make sure she really was seeing him. No real man was that… that… hell, she couldn't even think of an apt word to describe him. She shut her mouth quickly, before asking him to remove his shirt so she could see if his torso was really as gorgeous as she remembered while delirious.

"How are you feeling, Trinity?" He asked, the sound of his voice startling her out of her deer-in-the-headlights moment.

"Fine," she responded automatically. When someone asked how you were, that's just how you answered. She never thought about how stupid that was before. She was in a strange room in a foreign land with a complete stranger, and she said she was fine. She really was anything but, fine. What was even stranger was that alarm bells weren't ringing like they should be. She'd heard of tourists being snatched while in foreign lands, but she somehow didn't care.

Maybe she did have a head injury. The knot *was* pretty big. The only thing she seemed to care about was the food on the table, though.

"Are you hungry?" He asked her the one question she knew the answer to.

"Famished."

"Let's eat, then." He nodded to the chair he was holding out. Trinity's self-survival instincts finally seemed to kick in and she hesitated before walking closer to him.

"Where am I? Who are you? And why are we together?"

"You've been moved to the executive suite of the resort. My name is Drew, and I've been looking after you because you were hit on the head and couldn't stay alone," he answered matter-of-factly. His answers gave her enough comfort to finally sit. She should ask more, but her stomach just wouldn't stop growling. He laughed, which he quickly covered with a very poor cough imitation.

"I'm sorry, but I don't remember when I ate last," she said as she grabbed a pancake, rolled it up and ate it plain, which was her favorite way to them. Besides, she didn't have patience enough to spread butter and pour syrup. She couldn't remember ever being as hungry as she was at that moment.

"I was actually getting ready to wake you up when you came out. You've been asleep for fourteen hours," he answered.

No wonder she was so hungry. She'd gone straight to the beach the day before, without eating, then slept the entire rest of her day away.

"Why am I in the executive suite? There wasn't anything wrong with my room that I can remember."

"Because of your accident, the resort wanted to make your stay a lot more comfortable," he answered. Trinity looked at him, finding his tone a little odd. He seemed nervous, which she couldn't understand. Yeah, he'd hit her, but he hadn't been aiming for her. Accidents happened.

"I've never actually stayed in a room this nice," she said as excitement started building. She was disappointed when he looked around as if it wasn't anything new. Maybe he was used to luxury, but she wasn't.

"I ordered a little of everything because I didn't know what you'd like." Trinity was relieved when he broke the awkward silence.

"Thank you. The pancakes are great. So, I guess I wasn't swimming in the right place, huh? I didn't even see any surfers out there when I got in the water."

"Waves were really bad yesterday, not ideal for surfing, so there were only a couple tourists even trying. I was determined to find something, but then I hit you and…" Trinity burst into laughter, cutting Drew off. When he stared at her like she really did have a concussion and he should call the doctor, it caused her to laugh even harder.

"Sorry, really I am, but you have to admit it's pretty funny. I've never had a vacation before, ever, in my entire life. I'm always the good girl. I do everything right and always plays it safe, and then on my first day of vacation, I take a swim and get whacked in the head. It's pretty amusing," she said between fits of laughter. It seemed like the universe was telling her to be afraid to take adventures. Heck with that. She wasn't letting anything ruin her very pricy vacation.

"I do feel badly about the incident, and I apologize."

"Seriously, it's not like you jumped in the water and thought to yourself, *hmm I think I'd like to hit someone today,* so don't worry about it. After all, I did get this amazing suite and that's worth a nasty headache," she said. Trinity felt a bit of guilt over taking advantage of the situation. She really wasn't hurting. "I should tell them I'm not hurt, so they aren't worried. As much as I love the room, I don't want to lie to get it."

"I'm sure they're more than happy to let you stay here and recuperate fully. Why not enjoy the nice room, which also just happens to have the most spectacular view on the entire island. Live it up and have a great vacation," he told her.

"I'm too tired to even think about moving at the moment, so I'll have to think some more on it. What time is it anyway?" She asked.

"It's about five in the morning," he said with a yawn. "You slept the rest of the afternoon and most of the night."

"Wow, that's a bummer. I wasted an entire day of vacation. I'll just have to make up for it today," she said.

Drew knew he should just say goodbye and walk out the door. She was fine – she said so herself. She'd have a terrific vacation, on him, and never have to know. He couldn't seem to get his feet to move toward the door, though. He should run as fast as possible from the hotel, board his jet, and leave. He told himself he was going to do exactly that. He really intended to do just that, but somehow his tongue wouldn't listen to his brain.

"I'd love to be your tour guide," he offered. *No, no, no!* What was he thinking? He needed to get away from the woman causing his brain to be on permanent lock-down mode, not escorting her all over the island.

"Are you here on vacation too?" She asked.

"For now," he answered, telling her the partial truth. He'd come for a vacation, but it was only supposed to be for a few days, plus, it was his resort. He didn't want her to know. He found he didn't want to see the excited, almost innocent, light leave her eyes, to be replaced by greed. He'd yet to meet a woman who wasn't affected by the amount of money he had. He finally knew there was no fighting himself – he had to get to know Trinity – just enough to ease his curiosity. His vacation just got extended.

"In that case, I'd love to have a tour guide," she said before she stopped and looked at him with suspicion. He raised his brow at her questioningly.

"What do you do for a living?" She asked. He knew it was a test of some sort, but he didn't know what the right answer was. He didn't want to tell her the truth, but he also didn't want to stray too far from the truth. Once anyone started weaving lies, it was incredibly hard to break free from the web of deceit.

"I work for the resort," he finally answered. It was the truth, as he worked nonstop at the varying resorts.

"Oh, you work here. But you said you're on vacation," she said with a wrinkle back in place on her forehead. He needed to be careful not to chase her away.

"I'm off for a few days, which is always a vacation when you're in paradise," he answered. His answer seemed to be the right one because her face lit up and she went back to eating.

"In that case, I could most definitely use a guide, especially one who knows the area, but I don't want to take you away from your other activities," she said.

"Spending time with a beautiful lady is never a hardship." He gave her his most heart-stopping smile while he stuck his hand out so they could shake on it. He'd been told by more than one woman that his smile is what stopped them in their tracks. He wasn't above using everything in his arsenal to seduce Miss Trinity Mathews. And he knew that was his plan. It may be wrong of him, but he didn't care. He wanted her – the attraction was strong. He also noticed the way her eyes traveled along his body. She wanted him, too. She was just playing the game of chase – she wanted to be captured. He could feel it.

He watched Trinity hesitate as if she was afraid of touching him. She should be afraid. He could practically taste the sulfur in the air from all the sparks that were flying. Finally, she stuck out her hand. Drew smiled when he saw goose bumps appear on her arm. Oh yeah, he certainly affected her. His vacation was turning out quite well, so far.

Trinity quickly pulled away from him and dashed into the bedroom without saying another word. He heard the shower start a few moments later and decided it was a good time to call his staff. He told them no one was to approach him with any business. He didn't care if the building was on fire. He was officially on vacation and didn't want his guest to know he was the boss.

Right after he hung up the phone, it rang again. He saw the number was from his attorney and he reluctantly answered. He wasn't happy when he hung it back up. His attorney was faxing papers over and wanted to make sure Trinity signed them before the day was out. He was worried there'd be a huge lawsuit if she found out the person who had mowed her over was the owner of the resort. Drew wanted to tell the guy to stick it, but he was a good lawyer, and friend, who had never steered him wrong, not in the ten years Drew had known him.

Drew called the resort manager and asked him to handle the paperwork. He made sure they were going to comp her room, all meals, and any activities she did for the rest of the week. Ms. Mathews had earned an all-inclusive, free vacation. The attorney suggested a settlement of ten thousand dollars. Drew felt it was too small, but he'd see what her reaction was.

He prayed she didn't find out who he really was, because he had a feeling it really wouldn't go over well. In the meantime, he was going to give her the vacation of a lifetime.

When she returned from her shower, they headed downstairs.

"Ms. Mathews, can you step in here with me, please?" His manager approached them. Trinity looked at Drew with confusion. "I'm sorry, Ms. Mathews. I should've introduced myself. I'm Antony, the resort manager. I'd like to speak to you about yesterday and see if we can come up with a mutual agreement."

"Um, okay," Trinity nodded.

Drew stood and waited until she grabbed his hand. He hadn't wanted to go in with her, but he wasn't going to refuse her. He was curious what her reaction would be, though.

"We're very sorry about the incident yesterday. We take pride in our guests being taken care of better than at other less caring places. As you could see this morning, we've gone ahead and upgraded your room for the remainder of your stay. We've also credited back the payment for the week. All services at the hotel are on the house, and finally, we'd like to offer a settlement in the amount of ten-thousand dollars. All you need to do is sign this paper and it's a done deal. If you need anyone to look over it, that's fine, as well. We don't want to rush you."

Drew watched her face the entire time his manger spoke. She seemed in shock, confused, and a little hopeful, but he didn't see open greed enter her eyes. He waited to see what she would say.

"I'll sign your papers, promising not to sue, but you really don't need to give me all this. I'm feeling a little guilty about it. It wasn't as if Drew went out there trying to hurt me, and besides a small bump on my head, I'm fine. I don't even have the headache anymore," she said. It would be nice to take the money and enjoy a free vacation, but it wasn't their fault that Drew ran into her. It wasn't even Drew's fault. It was just one of those freak accidents.

"Trinity, corporations make massive amounts of money and can afford a small settlement like this. Besides, this is what insurance is for, right? Why don't you take what's being offered and have the vacation of a lifetime. Just think of all the spa services you can do," Drew said with his trust me smile on his face.

"You really think so?" She asked and he nodded. He waited anxiously as she turned back to the manager, who was nodding his encouragement, while holding out the pen. She finally took it and signed the papers. Drew let out a relieved breath. He wanted to get her away from the office and start his seduction plans. He had a full day of romance planned.

"We're sorry your vacation has been interrupted, and hope this will help make up for it. Please take advantage of all our services and fully enjoy your stay," Antony said.

"Thank you, you've been very kind. Maybe I'll use the money to go to one of your other resorts," she said, the idea seeming to excite her.

"That would be excellent, Ms. Mathews," Antony said. "If you decide to do that, give us a call and we'll make sure you get the royal service for a fraction of the cost," he finished.

Drew led her from the room and immediately steered her outside just as the sun was rising over the ocean. Even though it was early in the morning, it was still pleasantly warm so the two of them sat in the sand to enjoy the view.

Drew pulled her in front of him and wrapped her in his arms. He felt her stiffen as if she was struggling with the close contact. He didn't let go, but his grip was loose enough that she could pull away if she really wanted to. His heart pounded as he waited for her to decide what she was going to do. It seemed to be the moment that would decide the rest of the vacation. Would she be open to a fling? Or, was it too much for her?

When she finally relaxed and laid her head against his

chest, he had to fight the urge not to lay them both down on the sand and make love her right then with the sun rising over the ocean. Her presence alone was enough to send his body into overdrive, but when he touched her, it pushed him over the top. He knew he'd ever be able to look at a sunrise the same way again.

"What would you like to do next?" He whispered in her ear, making sure his breath caressed the sensitive skin. He was rewarded when a shiver racked her body. He rubbed his hand across her stomach, enjoying the feel of her quivering in his arms. He wanted to push further, but knew she was skittish. If he pressed too hard, too fast, he'd walk away unsatisfied.

"I told you earlier, this is my first vacation, so I'm going to leave it up to you. Whatever you think would be fun and adventurous," she mumbled as her head twisted against his shoulder and her eyes shut. He had to fight everything in him not to haul her back upstairs. There was only one fun and adventurous thing he wanted to do, and that involved them being in the bedroom, day and night.

"Okay, but be prepared for the consequences of leaving it all to me," he said. He had to quit playing the game he'd started, or he wouldn't be capable of walking anywhere. He slowly pulled his arms from around her, but nearly gave in to his desire when he heard the barest whimper escape her lips. She was just as turned on as him. He would spend the entire day building her body up, stroking her flames until she was ready to explode. By the time they did come together, the wait would be worth it. At least, that's what he told himself as he stood and then helped her to her feet.

###

The Tycoon's Vacation is available
now, at all major retailers.

Go to http://www.melodyanne.com to
add your email to Melody Anne's Mailing
List, and be notified of New Releases.

page intentionally left blank

7670410R50165

Made in the USA
San Bernardino, CA
14 January 2014